Dr Alessandro Lombardi strode into the crèche. He was tired. Dog-tired. Emotional upheaval, months of no sleep, moving to the other side of the planet and starting a new job had really taken their toll. He wanted to go home, get into bed and sleep for a year.

If only.

He pulled up short in the doorway as the sound of his son's laughter drifted towards him. It had been months since he'd heard the noise. He'd almost forgotten what it sounded like. And after an arduous day it was a surprising pick-me-up.

His midnight gaze followed the sound, widening to take in the picture before him: his son, cuddled up next to a woman with blonde hair and blue eyes. His fingers absently stroked her hair while he sucked his thumb, just as he'd used to do with his mother.

His welcoming smile froze before it had even made an indent into the uncompromising planes of his face. He crossed the room in three strides. 'Julian!'

Dear Reader

What is it about Italian men? Is it their dark, brooding looks, their seemingly effortless charisma, or that accent? Why are they so popular in our books? Why do we love to read about them so much? I'm not sure I know the reason myself, but I'm sure my two heroines Nat and Paige do!

When my editor suggested I write two linked books with Italian heroes I didn't hesitate. I've had such fun writing them in the past, how could I resist? And what fabulous men my muse presented to me!

Cousins Alessandro and Valentino Lombardi have so much in common—both specialist doctors, both compassionate and honourable men, growing up like brothers in Italy and forging new lives for themselves on the opposite side of the world. But also, in many ways, they are complete opposites. Alessandro, so strained and serious, failing to cope with the death of his wife and raising his four-year-old son. And Valentino, the fun-loving, easy-going Lothario.

It seemed only right to give them women they needed. Or who needed them. Nat, so bright and peppy, and determined to forge a bond between Alessandro and his son. And Paige, single mother of a deaf child, so fragile and shut down—a combination a hot-blooded Italian male like Valentino finds hard to resist.

I hope you enjoy their stories as these four special people find their way to love. I know I certainly enjoyed writing them.

I miss them already.

Love

Amy

ALESSANDRO AND THE CHEERY NANNY

BY
AMY ANDREWS

MILLS & BOON

First published in Great Britain 2010
Large Print edition 2011
Harlequin Mills & Boon Limited,
Eton House, 18-24 Paradise Road,
Richmond, Surrey TW9 1SR

© Amy Andrews

ISBN: 978 0 263 21723 0

Harlequin Mills & Boon policy is to use papers that are natural, renewable and recyclable products and made from wood grown in sustainable forests. The logging and manufacturing process conform to the legal environmental regulations of the country of origin.

Printed and bound in Great Britain
by CPI Antony Rowe, Chippenham, Wiltshire

Amy Andrews has always loved writing, and still can't quite believe that she gets to do it for a living. Creating wonderful heroines and gorgeous heroes and telling their stories is an amazing way to pass the day. Sometimes they don't always act as she'd like them to—but then neither do her kids, so she's kind of used to it. Amy lives in the very beautiful Samford Valley, with her husband and aforementioned children, along with six brown chooks and two black dogs. She loves to hear from her readers. Drop her a line at www.amyandrews.com.au

Recent titles by the same author:

This book is dedicated to
all good fathers and their sons.
Little boys need their daddies too.

CHAPTER ONE

NAT DAVIES was instantly attracted to the downcast head and the dark curly hair. There was something about the slump to the little boy's shoulders and the less than enthusiastic way he was colouring in. He seemed separate from the other children laughing and playing around him, and it roused the mother lion in her.

He was the only stationary object in a room full of movement. And he seemed so...forlorn.

'Who's that?' she asked, bumping Trudy's hip with hers to get her boss's attention.

Trudy stopped chopping fruit and followed Nat's gaze. 'Julian. It's his second day. Four years old. Father is ooh-la-la handsome. Italian. Perfect English. Just moved from London. Widower. Recent, I think. Doesn't smile much.'

Nat nodded, well used to Trudy's staccato style of speech. 'Poor darling.' No wonder he looked so bereft. 'How awful to lose your mother at such a young age.' Not that it mattered at any age really.

She'd been eight when her father had left and it still hurt.

Trudy nodded. 'He's very quiet. Very withdrawn.'

Nat's heart strings gave another tug. She'd always had a soft spot for loners. She knew how it felt to have your perfect world turned upside down while life continued around you. How alienating it could be. How it separated you from the bustle of life.

'Well, let's see if I can fix that,' she murmured.

Nat made a beeline for the lonely little boy, stopping only to grab a copy of *Possum Magic* off the bookshelf. In her experience she found there was very little a book couldn't fix, if only for a short while.

'Juliano.' Nat called his name softly as she approached, smiling gently.

The little boy looked up from his lacklustre attempt at colouring in a giant frog. His mouth dropped open and he stared at Nat with eyes that grew visibly rounder. She suppressed the frown that was itching to crease her forehead at the unexpected response. Surely he was used to hearing his name spoken in Italian?

He was looking at her with a mix of confusion

and wonder, like he was trying to figure out if he should run into her arms or burst into tears.

She kept her smile in place. *'Ciao*, Juliano. *Come sta?'*

Nat had learnt Italian at school and spent a year in Milan on a student exchange after completing grade twelve. Given that she was now thirty-three, it had been a while since she'd spoken it but she had been reasonably fluent at one stage.

Julian's grave little face eked out a tentative smile and Nat relaxed. *'Posso sedermi?'* she asked. Julian nodded and moved over so Nat could share the bench seat with him.

'Hi, Juliano. My name's Nat,' she said.

The boy's smile slipped a little. 'Papa likes me to be called Julian,' he said quietly.

The formality in his voice was heart-breaking and Nat wanted to reach out and give him a fierce hug. Four-year-olds shouldn't be so buttoned up. If this hadn't been St Auburn's Hospital crèche for the children of hospital staff, she might have wondered if Julian's father had a military background.

Maybe Captain Von Trapp. Before Maria had come on the scene.

'Julian it is,' she said, and held out her hand for a shake. He shook it like a good little soldier and the urge to tickle him until his giggles filled the room ate at her.

She battled very uncharitable thoughts towards the boy's father. Could he not see his son was miserable and so tightly wound he'd probably be the first four-year-old in history to develop an ulcer?

She reminded herself that the man had not long lost his wife and was no doubt grieving heavily. But his son had also lost his mother. Just because he was only four, it didn't mean that Julian wasn't capable of profound grief also.

'Would you like me to read you a story?' Nat pointed to the book. 'It's about a possum and has lots of wonderful Australian animals in it.'

Julian nodded. 'I like animals.'

'Have you got a pet?'

He shook his head forlornly. 'I had a cat. Pinocchio. But we had to leave him behind. Papa promised me another one but…he's been too busy…'

Nat ground her teeth. 'I have a cat. Her name's Flo. After Florence Nightingale. She loves fish and makes a noise like this.'

Nat mimicked the low rumbling of her five-year-old tortoiseshell, embellishing slightly. Julian giggled and it was such a beautiful sound she did it again. 'She's a purring machine.' Nat laughed and repeated the noise, delighted to once again hear Julian's giggle.

As children careened around them, immersed in their own worlds, she opened the book and began to read aloud, her heart warmed by Julian's instant immersion into its world. Page after page of exquisite illustrations of Australian bush animals swept them both away and by the end of the tale Julian was begging her to read it again, his little hand tucked into hers.

'I see you've made a friend there,' Trudy said a few minutes later, plonking a tray of cut-up fruit on the table in front of them and calling for the children to go and wash up for afternoon tea.

Julian followed the rest of the kids into the bathroom, looking behind him frequently to check Nat was still there. 'I hope so, Trude,' Nat replied.

If anyone needed a friend, it was Julian.

An hour later the chatter and chaos that was usually the kindy room was filled only with the beautiful sounds of silence as the busy bunch of three- to five-year-olds slumbered through the afternoon rest period. Nat wandered down the lines of little canvas beds, checking on her charges, pulling up kicked-off sheets and picking up the odd teddy bear that had been displaced.

She stopped at Julian's bed and looked down at his dear little face. His soft curls framed his cheeks and forehead. His olive complexion was flawless in the way of children the world over. His mouth had an enticing bow shape and his lips were fat little cherubic pillows.

Unlike every other child in the room, he slept alone, no cuddle toy clutched to his side. With the serious lines of his face smoothed in slumber he looked like any other carefree four-year-old. Except he wasn't. He was a motherless little boy who seemed to carry the weight of the world on his shoulders.

More like forty than four.

He whimpered slightly and his brow puckered. Her heart twisted and she reached out to smooth it but he turned on his side and as she watched, his thumb found its way into his mouth. He sucked subconsciously and her heart ached for him. He seemed so alone, even in sleep. It was wrong that a boy who had just lost his mother should have nothing other than a thumb to comfort him.

She made a mental note to talk to his father at pick-up. Ask him if Julian would like to bring along a toy, something familiar from home.

Maybe she could even broach the subject of counselling for Julian. Something had to be done for the sad little darling. Someone had to try.

It may as well be her.

It was early evening when Nat found herself curled up in a bean bag with Julian in Book Corner, reading *Possum Magic* for the third time. The room was once again quiet, most of the children having gone home, their parents' shifts long since finished. The few remaining kids had eaten their night-time meals and were occupied in quiet play.

Despite her best efforts to engage him with other children, Julian had steadfastly refused to join in, shadowing her instead. Nat knew she should be firmer but in a short space of time she'd developed a real soft spot for Julian.

His despondent little face clawed at her insides and she didn't have the heart to turn him away. He looked like he was crying out to be loved and Nat knew how that felt. How could she deny a grieving child some affection?

She didn't notice as she turned the pages that Julian's thumb had found its way into his mouth or that one little hand had worked its way into her hair, rhythmically stroking the blonde strands.

All she was really aware of was Julian's warm body pressed into her side and his belly laugh as she mimicked Grandma Poss and Hush on their quest to find the magic food. As ways to end the day went, it wasn't too bad at all.

Dr Alessandro Lombardi strode into the crèche. He was tired. Dog tired. Emotional upheaval, months of no sleep, moving to the other side of the planet and starting a new job had really taken their toll. He wanted to go home, get into bed and sleep for a year.

If only.

He pulled up short in the doorway as his son's laughter drifted towards him. It had been months since he'd heard the sound and he'd almost forgotten what it sounded like. And after an arduous day it was a surprising pick-me-up.

His midnight-dark gaze followed the sound, his eyes widening to take in the picture before him. His son cuddled up next to a woman with blonde hair and blue eyes exactly like Camilla's. His fingers absently stroked her hair while he sucked his thumb, just as he used to do with Camilla.

His welcoming smile froze before it had even made a dent into the uncompromising planes of his face. He crossed the room in three strides. 'Julian!'

Nat felt the word crack like a whip across the room and looked up startled as Julian's thumb fell from his mouth and he dropped his hand from her hair as if it had suddenly caught fire.

She didn't need Trudy to tell her Julian's father had arrived. They were carbon copies of each other. Same frowns, same serious gazes and brooding intensity, same cherubic mouths.

But where Julian's appeal was all round-eyed childhood innocence, his father's appeal was much more adult. There was nothing childish about his effect on her pulse. He looked like some tragic prince from a Shakespearean plot to whom the slings and arrows had not been kind.

Put quite simply, at one glance Julian's father was most categorically heart-throb material. A tumble of dark hair, with occasional streaks of silver, brushed his forehead and collar, a dark shadow drew the eye to his magnificent jaw line and that mouth…

She knew without a doubt she was going to dream about that mouth.

She suddenly felt warm all over despite the chill that blanketed her as cold dark eyes, like black ice, raked over her. Nat was used to men staring. She was blonde and, as had been pointed out to her on numerous occasions, had a decent rack. She was no supermodel but she knew she'd been blessed with clear skin, healthy hair and a perfect size twelve figure.

Until today she'd thought living in Italy had immunised her against being openly ogled. As an eighteen-year-old blonde with pale skin in a country where dark hair and olive complexions were the norm, she'd certainly attracted a lot of interest from Italian boys.

But there was nothing sexual about this Italian's interest. Rather he was looking at her like she was the wicked witch of the west.

And he was definitely no boy.

'Julian,' he said quietly, not taking his eyes off the strange woman who was eerily familiar. From the way she folded her long pale legs under her to the blonde ponytail that brushed her shoulders and the fringe that flicked back from her face, she was just like Camilla.

His gaze strayed to the way the top two buttons of her V-necked T-shirt gaped slightly across her ample chest. They lingered there for a moment, unconsciously appreciating the ripe swell of female flesh. It had been a long time since he'd appreciated a woman's cleavage and he quickly glanced away.

His gaze moved upwards instead, finding the similarities to Camilla slapped him in the face again. Same wide-set eyes, same high cheekbones, same full mouth and pointed chin complete with sexy little cleft that no doubt dimpled when she smiled.

Hell, he must be tired, he was hallucinating.

He held his hand out to his son. 'Come here.'

Julian obeyed his father immediately and Nat felt the beads of the bean bag beneath her shift and realign, deflating her position somewhat. She looked up, way up, at a distinct disadvantage in her semi-reclined state on the floor.

From this angle Julian's father looked even more intimidating. More male. His legs looked longer. His chest broader. He loomed above her and she was torn between professionalism and just lolling her head back and looking her fill.

She couldn't remember ever having such an immediate response to a man.

His pinstriped trousers fell softly against his legs, hinting at the powerful contours of his quadriceps. The thick fabric of his business shirt did the same, outlining broad shoulders and a lean torso tapering to even leaner hips.

Unfortunately he was still staring down at her like she was one of those insects who ate their young and reluctantly professionalism won out. She floundered in the bean bag for a few seconds, totally annihilating any chance of presenting herself as a highly skilled child care worker before struggling to her feet.

Snatching a moment to collect herself, she smiled encouragingly at Julian. She noticed immediately how, even standing next to his father, Julian still looked alone. They didn't touch. There had been no great-to-see-you hug, he didn't take his father's hand, neither did his father reach for him. There was no affectionate shoulder squeeze or special father-son eye contact.

It was obvious Julian wasn't frightened of him but also obvious the poor child didn't expect much.

Nat returned her gaze upwards. Good Lord— the man was tall. And seriously sexy. She smiled, mainly for Julian's benefit. 'Hi. I'm Nat Davies.' She extended her hand.

Alessandro blinked. He'd braced himself when she'd opened her mouth to speak, half expecting a cut-glass English accent. But when the words came out in that slow, laid-back Australian way, still unfamiliar to his ear, he relaxed slightly.

The similarities between this woman and his dead wife were startling on the surface. Same height, same build, same eye colour, same blonde hair worn in exactly the same style, same facial structure and generous mouth. Same cute chin dimple.

No wonder Julian had taken a shine to her.

But looking at the fresh-faced woman before him, he knew that's where the similarities ended. This woman exuded openness, friendliness, an innocence, almost, that his wife had never had.

Her hair had been dragged back into its band, rather hurriedly by the look of it, with strands wisping out everywhere. It hadn't been neatly coiffed and primped until every hair was in place.

And Camilla wouldn't have dared leave the house without make-up. This woman…Nat… was more the girl-next-door version of Camilla. Not the posh English version he'd married.

Even her perfume was different. Camilla had always favoured heavy, spicy perfumes that lingered long after she'd left the room. Nat Davies smelled like a flower garden. And…Plasticine. It was an intriguing mix.

Most importantly, her gaze was free of artifice,

free of agenda, and he felt instantly more relaxed around her then he ever had with Camilla.

Alessandro took the proffered hand and gave it a brief shake before extracting his own. 'Alessandro Lombardi.'

Nat blinked as the fleeting contact did funny things to her pulse. His voice was deep and rich like red wine and dark chocolate, his faint accent adding a glamorous edge to his exotic-sounding name. But the bronzed skin that stretched over the hard planes and angles of his face remained taut and Nat had the impression he wasn't given to great shows of emotion.

No wonder Julian rarely smiled if he lived with Mr Impassive. Nat looked down at Julian, who was inspecting the floor. 'Julian, matey, would you like to take *Possum Magic* home? It's part of our library. Maybe your papa could read it to you before bed tonight.'

Nat watched as Julian glanced hesitantly at his father, his solemn features heartbreakingly un-hopeful.

Alessandro nodded. *'Si.'*

Nat passed the book to Julian, who still looked grave despite his father's approval. Did he think perhaps his father wouldn't read him the book? She had to admit that Alessandro Lombardi didn't look like the cuddle-up-in-bed-with-his-son type. 'Go and find Trudy, matey. She'll show you how to fill out the library card.'

They watched Julian walk towards Trudy as if he was walking to his doom, clutching the book like it was his last meal.

Nat's gaze flicked back to Julian's father to find him already regarding her, his scrutiny as intense as before. 'Senor Lombardi, I was—'

'Mr, please,' he interrupted. Alessandro was surprised to hear the Italian address. Surprised too at the accuracy of her Italian accent. 'Or Doctor. Julian knows little Italian. His mother...' Alessandro paused, surprised how much even mentioning Camilla still packed a kick to his chest. 'His mother was English. It was her wish that it be his primary language.'

It was Nat's turn to be surprised. On a couple of counts. Firstly, Julian knew a lot more Italian than his father gave him credit for if today was anything to go by. And, secondly, what kind of mother would deny their child an opportunity to learn a second language—especially their father's native tongue?

But there was something about the way he'd faltered when he'd talked about his wife, the hesitation, the emptiness that prodded at her soft spot. He was obviously still grieving deeply. And maybe in his grief he was just trying to do the right thing by his dead wife? Trying to keep things going exactly as they had been for Julian's sake. Or desperately trying to hang onto a way of life that had been totally shattered.

On closer inspection she could see the dark smudges and fine lines around his eyes. He looked tired. Like he hadn't slept properly in a very long time.

Who was she to pass judgment?

'Dr Lombardi, I was wondering if Julian had a special toy or a teddy bear? Something familiar from home to help him feel a little less alone in this new environment?'

Alessandro stiffened. A toy. Of course, Camilla would have known that. There was that mangy-looking rabbit that he used to drag around with him everywhere. Somewhere…

'I've been very busy. Our things only arrived a few days ago and there's been no chance to unpack. We're still living out of boxes.'

Nat blinked. Too busy to surround your child with things that were familiar to him when so much in his world had been turned up-side down?

'This is none of my business, of course, but I understand you were recently widowed.'

Alessandro saw the softness in her eyes and wanted to yell at her to stop. He didn't deserve her pity. Instead, he gave a brief, controlled nod. '*Si.*'

If anything, he looked even bleaker than when he'd first entered but despite his grim face and keep-out vibes Nat was overwhelmed by the urge to pull them both close and hug them. Father and son. They'd been through so much and were both so obviously still hurting. She couldn't bear to see such sadness.

'I was wondering if Julian had had any kind of counselling.' *Or if the good doctor had, for that matter.* 'He seems quite…withdrawn. I can highly recommend the counselling service they run here through St Auburn's. The child psychologist is excellent. We could make an appointment-'

'You're right,' Alessandro interrupted for the second time, a nerve jumping at the angle of his jaw. 'This is none of your business.' He turned to locate his son. 'Come, Julian.'

Nat felt as if he had physically slapped her and she recoiled slightly. Alessandro Lombardi had a way with his voice that could freeze a volcano.

He was obviously unused to having his authority questioned.

She'd bet her last cent he was a surgeon.

She watched Dr Lombardi usher his son towards the door. Julian partially lifted his hand, reaching for his father's, then obviously thought better of it, dropping it by his side. He turned and gave her a small wave and a sad smile as he walked out the door, and Nat felt a lump swell in her throat.

They left side by side but emotionally separate. There was no picking his son up and carrying him out, not even a guiding hand on the back. Something, anything that said, even on a subliminal level, I love you, I'm here for you.

Nat hoped for Julian's sake that it was grief causing this strange disconnectedness between father and son and not something deeper. There was something unbearably sad about a four-year-old with no emotional expectations.

Having grown up with an emotionally distant father Nat knew too well how soul destroying it could be. How often had she'd yearned for his touch, his smile, his praise after he'd left? And how often had he let her down, too busy with his new family, with his boys? Even at thirty-three she was still looking for his love. She couldn't bear to see it happening to a child in her care.

But something inside her recognised that Alessandro Lombardi was hurting too. Knew that it was harsh to judge him. As a nurse she knew how grief affected people. How it could shut you down, cut you off at the knees. He had obviously loved his wife very deeply and was probably doing the best he could just to function every day.

To put one foot in front of the other.

Maybe he was just emotionally frozen. Not capable of any feelings at the moment. Maybe grief had just sucked them all away.

She sighed. It looked like she'd also developed a soft spot for the father also. Yep, it was official— she was a total sucker for a sob story.

The next day Nat had finished her stint in Outpatients and was heading back to the accident and emergency department for her very late lunch. She'd been sent there to cover for sick leave and was utterly exhausted.

She didn't mind being sent out of her usual work area and had covered Outpatients on quite a few occasions since starting at St Auburn's six months ago but it was a full-on morning which always ran over the scheduled one p.m. finish time. There hadn't been time for morning tea either so her stomach was protesting loudly. She could almost taste the hot meat pie she'd been daydreaming about for the last hour and a half.

Add to that being awake half the night thinking about Julian's situation, and she was totally wrecked. *And then there'd been the other half of the night.* Filled with images—very inappropriate images—of Julian's father and his rather enticing mouth.

She'd known she was going to dream about that mouth.

'Oh, good, you're back. I need another experienced hand,' Imogen Reddy, the nurse in charge, said as Nat wandered back. 'It's Looney Tunes here. Code one just arrived in Resus. Seventy-two-year old-male, suspected MI. Can you get in and give the new doc a hand? Delia's there but she was due off half an hour ago and hasn't even had time for a break. Can you take over and send her home?'

Nat looked at the bedlam all around her. *Just another crazy day at St Auburn's Accident and Emergency.* And they wondered why she kept knocking back a full-time position. Nat's stomach growled a warning at her but she knew there was no way she could let a seven-months-pregnant colleague do overtime on an empty stomach.

She smiled at her boss. 'Resus. Sure thing.'

Nat stopped just outside the resus cubicle and pulled a pair of medium gloves out of a dispenser attached to the wall. She snapped them on, took a deep breath, flicked back the curtain and entered the fray.

'Okay, Delia. You're off,' she said, smiling at her colleague who happened to be the first person she saw amidst the chaos. 'Go home, put your feet up and feed the foetus.'

Delia shoulders sagged and she gave Nat a grateful smile. 'Are you sure?' She turned and addressed the doctor. 'Are you okay if I go, Alessandro? You're getting a much better deal. Nat here is Super-Nurse.'

Alessandro? Nat swung around to find Alessandro Lombardi, all big and brooding, behind her. The bustle, the sounds of the oxygen and the monitors around her faded out as she stared into those coalpit-black eyes.

They were alert, radiating intelligence, but if anything he looked more tired than he had yesterday. He stared back and Nat felt as if she was naked in front of him.

She dropped her gaze as some of the images

from last night's dream revisited. *Bloody hell. He was the new doctor?* Working part-time generally kept Nat out of the loop with medical staff rotations and she'd just assumed Imogen had meant a new registrar. Surely Julian's father was a little too old to be a registrar?

So much for her surgeon theory.

Alessandro took in the woman who had been the cause of another sleepless night. A new cause, granted, but still a complication he didn't need. She was different today, out of her shorts and T-shirt. Very professional looking in the modest white uniform with the zip up the front. Her hair was a little neater in her ponytail and in this environment he felt on a more even keel around her.

Still, his gaze dropped to the zip briefly and before he could stop it, an image of him yanking the slider down flitted across his mind's eye.

He looked at Delia briefly. 'Yes. We've met.'

Then he turned back to the patient and Nat felt thoroughly dismissed. If only he knew what he'd done to her in her dreams last night…

Had she had time she might have been miffed but her patient caught her attention. 'Super-Nurse, hey?' he croaked behind his oxygen mask.

Nat dragged her gaze away from the back of Alessandro's head to look at the patient. He was sweaty and grey with massive ST changes on his monitor. Multiple ectopic beats were worrying and as she watched, a short run of ventricular tachycardia interrupted his rhythm.

His heart muscle was dying.

He was also in pain despite the morphine that she noted had already been administered, but there was still a twinkle visible in his bright eyes. He was obviously one of those stoic old men who didn't believe in complaining too much.

'Yes, sir.' She reached for his hand and gave it a squeeze. 'That's me. To the rescue.'

The patient gave a weak chuckle. 'Ernie,' he puffed out. 'Looks like I'm in safe hands, then.'

Nat glanced at Alessandro. She hoped so. She hoped he was better at doctoring than he was at communicating. At fathering. 'The very best.'

'What's the ETA on the CCU docs?' Alessandro asked no one in particular.

Seeing Nat Davies from the crèche was a bit of a surprise but he didn't have time to ponder that, or her damn zip, now. He had to focus on his patient, who needed that consult and admission to the coronary care unit pronto.

Ernie's ECG was showing a massive inferior myocardial infarction. They were administering the right drugs to halt the progress of the heart attack but these patients were notoriously unstable and with age against him, Alessandro worried that Ernie would arrest before the drugs could work. Or that his heart was already too damaged.

'Couple of minutes,' someone behind him said.

As it turned out, Ernie didn't have a couple of minutes and Alessandro's worst fears were realised when the monitor alarmed and Ernie lost consciousness.

'VF,' Nat announced as the green line on the screen developed into a series of frenetic squiggles. Her own heart rate spiked as a charge of adrenaline shot through her system like vodka on an empty stomach.

Alessandro pointed at Nat. 'Commence CPR. I'll intubate. Adrenaline,' he ordered. 'Charge the defib.'

Nat hiked the skirt of her uniform up her thighs a little as she climbed up onto the narrow gurney. She planted her knees wide and balanced on the edge of the mattress, a feat she'd performed a little too often, as she started compressions.

Any ill will she may have been harbouring towards Dr Lombardi fizzled in an instant at the totally professional way he ran the code. It was textbook. But that wasn't doing him justice. It was more than textbook. He didn't see a seventy-two-year-old man and give up after a few minutes. He gave Ernie every chance. It wasn't until the down time reached thirty minutes that he finally called it.

He placed his hands on Nat's, stilling their downward trajectory. 'Thank you,' he said. Then he looked at the clock. 'Time of death fifteen twenty-two hours.'

Nat looked down at his hands. She could just see her own through the gloved fingers of his. She noticed for the first time his sleeves were rolled back to reveal the dark hair of his bronzed forearms and she absently thought how strong they looked. How manly.

She glanced at him and their eyes locked, a strange solidarity uniting them. She could see the impact of this loss in his bleak stare. As she watched, his gaze drifted briefly south, lapping her cleavage, and she felt her nipples bead as if he'd actually caressed them. When he looked back at her, all she could see was heat.

Two beats passed and then as quickly as the heat had come it disappeared and he was removing his hands, extending one to help her off the gurney.

Dragging her gaze from him, she accepted, easing back to the floor.

Her knees nearly buckled and Nat snatched her hand away, grabbing for the edge of the trolley to steady herself.

'Are you okay?' he asked as he watched her wobble slightly.

Nat rubbed her at her knees. 'Fine'

Except, staring down at Ernie, she knew it wasn't. Ernie was dead. And whatever was going on between her and Alessandro didn't matter next to that. Neither did it matter that she'd only known Ernie for only a handful of minutes—he was still dead. Gone. The twinkle in his eyes extinguished for ever. In fact, it made it worse that she didn't know him. It was wrong that a person should die surrounded by strangers.

She felt as she always did, overwhelmingly sad.

Alessandro nodded. 'We need to talk to his family.'

His cold onyx gaze bored into hers with an air of expectation, no trace of the heat from a moment ago.

Looked like she was going with him.

Confronted with the businesslike professional, she wondered if she'd imagined the fleeting glimpse of sorrow and passion she'd seen. Her tummy growled again and she bargained with it for another half an hour.

Alessandro strode briskly ahead and Nat worried as she followed him. Sure, the view was good. His trousers hugged the tight contours of his butt and each stride emphasised not only the power of his legs but pulled at his shirt, emphasising the broadness of his back.

But none of that meant this man was remotely equipped to talk to grieving relatives. He was still grieving himself. Had Ernie's death resonated with him? Had this death reminded him of his dead wife, of his own grief?

He was obviously a consultant, she didn't think for a moment this was his first time. But if he was as emotionally disconnected with this family as he was with his son, it could be disastrous for them. As a nurse she was used to being involved in these conversations but did he only want her there to fill in the emotional gaps for him? Was she going to be left to pick up the pieces like she'd done too many times before in her career because too often doctors were ill equipped for this sort of situation?

She contemplated saying something. But despite the brief flare of desire that had licked her with heat, his terse *This is none of your business* from yesterday still rang in her ears and she didn't want to annoy him before this heart-wrenching job. But he seemed as tense as yesterday, as distant, and not even the growling of her stomach could override the foreboding that shadowed her as she tried to keep up with his impossibly long stride.

Telling someone their husband/child/mother/ significant other had died was always dreadful. As a health-care worker, Nat would rather clean bedpans all shift than witness the devastating effects of those awful few words. But she knew Ernie's wife and kids deserved the truth and she knew they'd have questions that only someone who had been there could answer.

And that was her.

She couldn't back away from that. No matter how much she wanted to.

Much to her surprise, Alessandro again totally confounded her. He spoke softly, his accent more apparent as he gently outlined what had happened and how they'd tried but in the end there had been nothing they could do to bring Ernie back. The family cried and got angry and asked questions and Alessandro was calm and gentle and patient.

He was compassion personified.

And at the end when Ernie's wife tentatively put out her hand to bridge the short distance between Alessandro and herself and then thought better of it and withdrew it, it was he who reached out and took her hand.

It should have melted her marshmallow heart in an instant. But it didn't.

It reminded her of yesterday and Julian reaching for his father's hand and it had the opposite effect. She was furious. It felt like a red-hot poker had been shoved through her heart. She wasn't sure if it was the lack of food or the lack of sleep but she felt irrationally angry.

Was this man schizophrenic? Was he some sort of Jekyll and Hyde? How could he offer Ernie's wife, a relative stranger, the comfort he denied his own child?

He'd shown this family, this previously unknown collection of people, more sensitivity, more emotion, than he'd displayed for his four-year-old son. Yesterday she'd thought he was emotionally crippled. Grieving for his wife. Today, as they'd walked to do this, she'd worried about it again. Worried about his ability to empathise when he was buried under the weight of his own grief.

But it wasn't the case. He was obviously a brilliant emergency physician with a fabulous bedside manner. He just didn't take it home with him. To the most important person in the world. To his own child. To his son.

They left Ernie's family after about twenty minutes and Nat had never been more pleased to be shed of a person in her life. She steamed ahead, knowing if she didn't get away from him she would say something she would regret.

Alessandro frowned as Nat forged ahead. She seemed upset and as much as he didn't want anything to do with the woman who could almost have been Camilla's twin, they worked together and he knew that sudden death, such as they'd both just been part of, took its toll.

He caught her up. 'Are you okay?'

'Fine.' She repeated her response from earlier.

Except she wasn't. It didn't take a genius to figure out that something was bothering her. He grabbed her arm to prevent her walking away any further. 'I don't think you are.'

Nat looked at his bronzed hand on her pale arm. She looked at him. *Oh, Senor, you really don't want to mess with me now.* She pulled her arm away but he tightened his grip.

Heat radiated from his hand and spread up her

arm to her breasts and belly. Damn it, she did not want to feel like this. Not now. She was mad. *Furious*. She sucked in a breath, ragged from her brisk walk and the rage bubbling beneath the surface.

They were standing in the corridor facing each other and it was as if time stood still around them and they were the only two people on the planet. Nat couldn't believe how it was possible to want to shake someone and totally pash their lips off at the same time.

'I'm fine.' The denial was low and guttural.

Alessandro could see the agitated rise and fall of her chest, see the colour in her cheeks. His gaze drifted to her mouth, her parted lips enticing.

He dragged his gaze away. 'I don't believe you. I know these cases can be difficult—'

Nat's snort ripped through his words and gave her mouth something else to do other than beg for his kiss. 'You think this is about Ernie?' She stared into his handsome face, at his peppered jaw line. How could she want someone who was so bloody obtuse?

'It's not?'

Nat snorted again and she knew she couldn't hold it back any longer. 'Tell me, how is it that you can reach out and hold a stranger's hand

and yet you can't offer your own son the same comfort?'

Alessandro froze at the accusation in her words. He dropped his hand from her arm as if he'd suddenly discovered she was suffering from the ebola virus. Nat watched his black ice eyes chill over as he paled beneath his magnificent bronze complexion. But she was on a roll now and she'd come this far.

'Nothing to say?' she taunted.

'Oh, I think you've said enough for both of us. Don't you?'

And before she knew it he'd turned on his heel, his rapidly departing figure storming along the corridor ahead.

She sucked in a breath, her body quivering from anger and something else even more primitive. She guessed she should feel chastised but she couldn't. If he could show this level of compassion at work, even if it was just an act, he sure as hell could show it at home.

If she could save Julian from the emotional wasteland she'd trodden, trying to please her father throughout her childhood, then she would. Attraction or no attraction.

So, no. She hadn't said enough. Not nearly enough. Not by a long shot.

CHAPTER TWO

Two weeks later Brisbane was in the throes of an unremitting heatwave. The power grid couldn't keep up with consumer demand for ceiling fans and 24-hour-a-day air-conditioning. Tempers were short. Road rage, heat stroke and dehydration were rampant.

Even in a city that regularly sweltered each summer, the temperatures were extreme. But this was spring and totally ironic when the other side of the world battled the looming pandemic of a horrible new strain of influenza and unseasonal snow was causing general havoc.

Nat actually looked forward to stepping through the doors of St Auburn's and being enveloped in a cool blast of air. Anywhere was better than her hot little box the real estate agent euphemistically called a townhouse in a breezeless suburb blistering beneath the sun's relentless rays.

Not that it would matter soon, seeing that it looked like she was going to be evicted by the end of the month.

Nat stepped into the crowded lift on the eighth floor, pondering this conundrum yet again. She'd just transferred another heat-stroke victim to the medical ward and was returning to the department. She squeezed in and, noting the ground-floor button had already been pushed, let her mind wander to the phone call she was expecting from the realtor any time now. She would find out today whether she could get an extension on her lease.

It wasn't until the lift emptied out over the next few floors and she had some more room to move that she was even aware of her fellow travellers. Two more people got out at the fourth floor and she was suddenly aware of there being only one other person left. Big and looming behind her. A strange sixth sense, or possibly foreboding, settled around her and she glanced quickly over her shoulder.

Alessandro Lombardi stared back at her, one dark eyebrow quirked sardonically. *Hell.* She had only seen him very briefly and at a distance in the last couple of weeks since she'd basically accused him of being a terrible father. He was wearing a pale lemon shirt and a classy orange tie. A stethoscope was slung casually around his neck.

In short he was looking damn fine and her hormones roared to life.

She turned back to the panel, pressing 'G' several times as the door slowly shut, her heart beating double time.

A fleeting smile touched Alessandro's mouth as he stared at her back, her blonde ponytail brushing her collar. It was the first time he'd been close to her since her outburst a little while ago. But he'd certainly heard her name frequently enough. Julian had spoken of little else. He'd heard it so often he'd started to dream about her.

He moved to stand beside her. 'Good afternoon, Nat.'

Nat took a steadying breath. 'Dr Lombardi,' she said, refusing to turn and face him. She jabbed at the 'G' several more times—why was this lift so damn slow?

'Be careful. You'll break it.'

She could detect a faint trace of amusement in his voice but today with the heat and the eviction hanging over her head she really wasn't in the mood. She hit it one more time for good measure.

Which was when the lift came to a grinding halt, causing her to stumble against him. She heard him mutter *'Porca vacca'* as he was jostled towards her and she supposed, absently, a profanity was better than an *I told you so.*

His hand cupped her elbow and the lights flickered out. It was a few seconds before either of them moved or spoke. Alessandro recovered first.

'Are you okay?'

His big hand was warm on her arm and for a second she even leaned into him, her pulse skipping madly in her chest as her body tried to figure out what was the bigger problem. Being stuck in a lift. Or being stuck in a lift with Alessandro Lombardi.

'You know,' she said, moving her elbow out of his grasp, 'when they teach you a foreign language it's always the swear words you learn first?'

Alessandro chuckled. 'Guilty.'

His low laughter sounded strange coming from a man who had thus far looked incapable of anything remotely joyous. But it enveloped her in the darkness and made her feel curiously safe.

The lights flickered on, or at least one of them did, and Alessandro braced himself for the lift to power up and lurch to a start. When nothing happened he looked down at Nat, who was looking expectantly at the ceiling. He hadn't realised they were standing so close.

Her flower-garden scent wafted towards him and when her gaze shifted from surveying the ceiling to meet his, the urge to move closer, to stroke his finger down her cheek, was a potent force.

He took a step back. His attraction to this woman was a complication he didn't need. 'I'll ring and see what's happened.'

Nat nodded absently, also backing up, pleased to feel the solidness of the wall behind her. For a moment there, maybe it had been the half-light, his eyes had darkened even further and she could have sworn he was going to touch her. *In a good way.*

She felt as if there wasn't enough air suddenly and took some calming breaths. She wasn't the hysterical type and now was not the time to become one.

Nat listened absently as Alessandro had a conversation with someone on the other end of the lift's emergency phone. It was brief and from the tone it didn't sound like they were getting out any time soon.

He hung up the phone and turned to her. 'There's a problem with the city grid. Something to do with the heat wave. The emergency power has kicked in but two lifts have failed to start. They're working on it.'

Nat licked her lips, the thought of spending time with him in a confined space rather unsettling. Did he also feel the buzz between them or was it all one sided? 'Did they have any idea how long it might take?'

'No.'

'*Porca vacca*,' she muttered, figuring Alessandro's instinctive expletive was as good as any. In either language.

Alessandro suppressed another chuckle. He could see her gaze darting around the lift and he wondered if she was trying to calculate carbon-dioxide build-up or was looking for an escape hatch. 'You're not claustrophobic, I hope?'

Nat shook her head. 'No. I'm afraid you'll be disappointed if you're waiting for me to turn into a hysterical female.'

Was he disappointed? Certainly Camilla would have thrown her first tantrum by now, demanding to speak to someone in authority. He much preferred Nat's calm resignation. 'Good.'

Nat glanced at him briefly and quickly looked away. He loomed in the dim light and with each passing second he seemed to take up more room.

'Well, no point in standing. Might as well get comfortable for the long haul.'

She sat then, cross-legged on the floor, her back pressed to the wall. She looked up at him looking down at her and was reminded of their first meeting when she'd had the bean-bag disadvantage. He was looking at her with that now familiar coolness in his eyes.

'Sit down, for God's sake,' she grouched.

Alessandro frowned. Nat Davies was one bossy little package. He slid down the wall, planting his feet evenly in front of him, his knees bent. 'Are you always this disagreeable?'

Nat, who was excruciatingly aware of his encroaching masculinity, shot him a startled look. She opened her mouth to protest. No, she wasn't. Despite her father's desertion and the recent ending of a long-term messy relationship that would have caused the most congenial woman to become a bitter hag, she was essentially a very agreeable person.

Perennially happy. Everyone said so. She almost told him so too. But then a quick review of the twice she'd spoken to him had her conceding that his comment was probably fair.

She raised her gaze from the very fascinating way his trousers pulled across his thigh muscles.

'I owe you an apology. For the other day. After Ernie. I was out of line. It was none of my business.'

Alessandro was surprised by her admission. It was refreshing to be with a woman who could apologise. 'You did overstep the line a little.'

Nat wanted to protest again, justify her reaction as being in Julian's interests, but he was right. 'I get too involved. I always have. The matron where I trained said I was a hopeless case.'

Alessandro smiled grudgingly. He removed his stethoscope and loosened his tie. It was already starting to get stuffy without the benefit of the air-conditioning. 'There are worse human flaws.'

He knew that only too well.

Nat stared at how even a small lift to his beautiful mouth transformed his face. Combined with the now skew tie and the undone top button, revealing a tantalising glimpse of very male neck, he really was a sight to behold. She smiled back. 'She didn't think so.'

Alessandro straightened a leg, stretching it out in front of him. He shrugged, looking directly at her. 'We'd just lost the battle to save a man's life. Death affects everyone in different ways.'

The teasing light she'd glimpsed briefly snuffed out and he seemed bleak and serious again. An older version of Julian. She hesitated briefly before voicing the question that entered her head. But they had to talk about something. And maybe he was looking for an opening? 'How long ago did your wife die?'

Alex felt the automatic tensing of the muscles in his neck. A fragment of a memory slipped out unbidden from the steel trap in his brain. Opening his door on the other side of the world to two grim-looking policemen. He drew his leg up again.

Nat watched him withdraw, startled by a twist of empathy deep inside.

Oh, no. No. No. No.

Alessandro Lombardi was a big boy. He didn't need her empathy. It was bad enough that she was sexually attracted to him. He didn't need her to comfort him and fix things too. His wife was dead—she couldn't fix that. Only time could fix that.

'I'm sorry. There I go again. None of my business.'

No. It wasn't. But he was damned if he wasn't opening his mouth to tell her anyway. 'Nine months.'

Nat was surprised. Both that he had responded and by the nine months. She'd known it was recent but it was still confronting. No wonder they were both so raw. 'I'm so very sorry,' she murmured.

Alessandro watched as her gaze filled with pity, the blue of her irises turning soft and glassy in the gentle light. He couldn't bear to see it. A sudden black fury streaked through him fast and hot like a lightning bolt from the deep well of self-hatred that bubbled never far from the surface. He didn't deserve her pity. He wasn't worthy of it. All he deserved was her contempt.

This was why he'd left England. To get far away from other people's pity. Their well-meaning words and greeting-card platitudes. Knowing that he had driven her to her death, that he alone was responsible…the hypocrisy had eaten him up inside.

Looking into Julian's face every day was more than he could stand. It was much easier not to.

He dropped his gaze. It took all of his willpower to drag himself back from the storm of broiling emotions squeezing his gut. 'Nat,' he said to the floor, before raising his face to meet hers, 'is that short for something?'

There had been a moment, before he'd looked down, when she'd glimpsed a heart-breaking well of despair. But it was shuttered now, safely masked behind a gaze that could have been hewn from arctic tundra.

He was obviously still deeply in love with his wife. It was also obvious he wasn't going to talk about it with her.

'Natalie,' she said, taking the not-so-subtle hint. 'I was supposed to be a boy.'

'Ah.'

'Nathaniel. Nat for short.'

She told the story she knew off by heart, careful not to betray how inadequate it made her feel. How she'd never felt like she quite measured up because her father had wanted a boy. 'My parents had kind of got used to thinking of me as Nat so they decided on Natalie.'

'Nathalie.' Alessandro rolled the Italian version round his tongue. 'It's pretty. Much prettier than Nat.'

It certainly was when he said it. His accent made a *th* pronunciation shading it with an exotic sound plain old Nat never had. Coming from his lips it sounded all grown up. No girl-next-door connotation. No one-size-fits-all, unisex, if-only-you'd-been-a-boy name.

In one breath he'd feminised it.

And right then, sitting on the floor in the gloom of a broken-down lift, she could see how women fell in love at first sight. Not that she was quite that stupid. Not any more. After Rob she knew better than to get involved with a man who was in love with another woman. Even a dead one.

But raw heat coated her insides and she squirmed against the floor to quell the sticky tentacles of desire.

'I prefer Nat,' she dismissed lightly, brushing at imaginary fluff on her skirt.

Alessandro dropped his eyes, watching the nervous gesture. It was preferable to the vulnerability he'd seen in her unmasked gaze.

'Ah, yes, Nat. Nat, Nat, Nat. I hear that name so often at home these days I'm beginning to think you must have magical powers. I think you could give Harry Potter a run for his money.'

Nat, pleased to be off more personal subjects, laughed out loud. Right. If she had magical powers she sure as hell would have used them shamelessly to her advantage long before now. Made her father love her more. Made Rob love her more. Made them stay.

'Julian talks about me?'

Despite not wanting to, Alessandro noticed the way her uniform pulled across her chest. The way the slide nestled in her cleavage. It had been such a long time since he'd noticed anything much about a woman at all but it was becoming a habit with this bossy, talkative Australian nurse.

He sent her a tight smile. 'Nonstop.'

Nat grinned. 'Sorry.' But she really wasn't. It made her happy to think she was making a difference to the serious little boy who came to the crèche. She knew she looked out for him on her days there and her heart melted faster than an ice-cube in this damn heat wave, when his sad little face lit up like a New Year's Eve firework display the moment he spotted her.

Alessandro shrugged. 'I'm pleased he…has someone.' Even if hearing her name incessantly meant she was never far from his thoughts. Even if that transferred into the rare moments of sleep he managed to snatch during nights that seemed to last an eternity. Those few precious hours were suddenly full of her. Bizarre erotic snapshots the likes of which he hadn't experienced since puberty.

Just another reason to despise himself a little bit more. Camilla hadn't even been dead a year and he was fantasising about some…look-alike-but-not Australian bossy-boots, like a horny teenager.

'He's a great kid, Alessandro.'

Her voice had softened and he could tell she

held genuine affection for Julian. He wished his own relationship with his son was as un-complicated. When he looked at Julian he saw Camilla and his guilt ratcheted up another notch. 'I know.'

And he did know. But he didn't know how to reach a child who was a stranger to him. He didn't know how to look at his son, love his son and pretend that he wasn't the reason Julian's world had been torn apart.

Perhaps if they'd been closer…

They looked at each other for a long moment, the air thick between them with things neither of them were game enough to say aloud. A phone ringing broke the compelling eye contact and it took a few seconds for Nat to realise it wasn't the lift emergency phone but her mobile.

She pulled it out of her pocket. 'Huh, look at that,' she mused. 'Good reception. Go figure.' She looked at the number on the screen and gave an inward groan. Great timing.

It was difficult for Alessandro not to eavesdrop. It was impossible to even pretend he wasn't. There was him and her in a tiny metal box, not much light and nothing else to do. He did try to feign disinterest, pulling his pager out and deleting the build-up of stored messages, but it was obvious she was having problems with her lease.

When Nat pushed the 'end' button on her phone with a grimace he said, *'Problemo?'*

Nat sighed and stuffed the phone back in her pocket. 'You could say that.'

'Sounds like you're having trouble with your landlord.'

Nat gave a derisive snort. 'That's an understatement. I've been given two weeks to move out.'

Alessandro dropped both of his legs, stretching them out in front as he crossed his arms across his chest. 'Let me guess. You have lots of loud parties and are behind on your rent?'

Nat, aware that his legs were a good deal closer now, flicked him a *funny ha-ha* look. The fact that he was even attempting humour wasn't enough to lift her out of the doldrums.

Where the hell was she going to go? 'The owners want to move back in.'

'Can they do that?'

Nat shrugged. 'The lease is up.'

'Ah.'

She sighed. 'Yes. Ah.'

'Have you thought of buying? It's a buyers' market at the moment with the world economic situation and interest rates being at an all-time low. I bought my place in Paddington for a very good price.'

'I have bought a place. A unit not far from St Auburn's. I bought it off the plan. It was supposed to be finished two months ago but with all that winter rain we had it's behind schedule.'

'Ah.'

Nat's legs were starting to cramp in her cross-legged position so she also stretched her legs out, her modest uniform riding up a little and revealing two very well-defined kneecaps and a hint of thigh. 'I only took a six-month lease because the project manager assured me the project would be on time. Damn man is as slippery as an oily snake.'

Alessandro's gaze dropped to the narrow strip of thigh visible between her knees and hemline before he realised what he was doing. He dragged his attention back to her frowning face. 'Do you not have a man, a husband or boyfriend, who can deal with these things for you?'

If she hadn't already been annoyed at the world—heat wave, broken lift, difficult land-lord—Nat might have laughed at his typical Italian male assumptions. But unfortunately for Alessandro, she was.

'I don't need a *man* to deal with stuff for me,' she said sharply.

Frankly she was sick of men. It was because of a bloody man she was in this pickle to start with. Eternal spinsterhood was looking like a damn fine alternative these days. Although the presence of a six-foot-nine Neanderthal next time she visited her half-complete unit did hold some appeal.

Alessandro held up his hands in surrender, not wanting to get into a debate about gender roles with her already looking like she was spoiling for a fight. Things were different these days, which was a good thing. And this wasn't Italy. Besides, they might well need to preserve oxygen.

'Have you not got family here you can stay with?'

She shook her head. 'All my family live in Perth. In Western Australia. I've only been in Brisbane for six months.'

'You are a long way from home, Nathalie.'

His voice was low and it slithered across the floor of the lift like a serpent, inching up her leg, under her skirt, gliding across her belly and undulating up her spine, stroking every hot spot in between. She was one giant goose-bump in three seconds flat.

The ease with which he accomplished it was shocking but she was damned if she was going to let her body do the talking. She raised an eyebrow, going for sardonic. '*I'm* a long way from home?'

He chuckled. *Well deflected. 'Touché.'* There were a few moments of silence as they both contemplated the floor. Alessandro had the feeling there was more to the Nat Davies story. He checked his watch. Ten minutes. How much longer?

It seemed stupid to sit in silence.

'So why did you leave Perth? Was there a reason or did you have a crashing desire to see Queensland?'

Nat gave a nonchalant shrug. 'I had a fancy to see the sun rise over the ocean.'

Alessandro smiled at her flippant reply. He was pretty sure it ran deeper than that. It took one damaged soul to recognise another. 'I get the feeling there may have been a man involved?'

Nat contemplated another snappy quip but she'd never been able to pull flippant off for very long. 'There was.'

'What happened?'

Nat repeated her earlier eyebrow rise. 'I think

this is where I tell you it's none of your business, isn't it?'

Alessandro nodded his head, a small smile playing on his lips. 'I do believe so, yes.' He shrugged. 'Just trying to pass the time.'

Nat regarded him for a few moments. Why did she feel so compelled to talk to him? One look at him and she lost her mind. She didn't bother to point out they could pass it just as easily by talking about his stuff because frankly she was tired of listening to men talk about women who used to share their lives.

'It became…untenable.' She waited for the barb in her chest to twist again, like it always did when she thought about Rob and their crazy crowded relationship. Her, him and his ex-wife.

Curiously it didn't.

Alessandro nodded. So they were both running away…

'So I left. I didn't plan to leave Perth but then I hadn't planned on it being so hard to still move in the same circles.'

She glanced at him, wondering what he was thinking, wondering if he empathised. Was that why he'd moved to the other side of the world? To escape the memories that were there, waiting around every corner? 'When the property settlement came through I just…left. Took my half and relocated.'

Alessandro nodded. 'That took courage.' He knew how hard it was to up sticks.

'Yeah, well, it doesn't seem so brave now, does it?'

Alessandro crossed one outstretched leg over the other at the ankles. 'Do you have a plan B?'

'The rental market in Brisbane is tight. I only need a couple of months but no one's going to be keen to rent to me for such a short time.'

Alessandro nodded. He'd tried to get a short-term lease so he didn't have to rush into buying but there'd been nothing available and he'd taken the plunge and bought instead.

'I don't really know anyone well enough to crash with them for long periods of time, apart from Paige who I went to school with in Perth. She works in Audiology and part time in the operating theatres at St Auburn's. I stayed with her for a couple of weeks when I first arrived but her husband walked out over two years ago and she has a three-year-old with high needs. I can't impose on them again.' She shrugged. 'The short answer is, I don't know. But something will show up. It'll work out, it always does.'

As soon as the words were out the lights flickered on in the lift and the air-conditioning whirred to life. Nat laughed. 'See?'

Alessandro smiled, picking up his pager and stethoscope off the floor as the lift shuddered and began its descent. He vaulted to his feet and held out a hand to her. She hesitated for a fraction and then took it. He pulled her up, the lift settling on the ground floor as she rose to her feet, causing her to stumble a little.

Nat put her hand against his chest to steady herself, aware that his other arm had come around to help. She copped a lungful of something spicy and for a brief dizzying second she considered pushing her nose into the patch of neck his skew tie had revealed to see if she could discern the exact origin. His lips were close and his gaze seemed to be suddenly fixed on her mouth and all she could think about was kissing him.

His heart thudded directly below her palm and the vibrations travelled down her arm, rippling through every nerve ending in her body, energising every cell.

The lift dinged and saved her from totally losing her mind. 'Oops, sorry,' she said, pushing away from him, uncharacteristic colour creeping into her cheeks.

The doors opened and a small crowd of maintenance people as well as department staff were there to greet them, clapping and cheering.

Nat risked a quick glance at him, dismayed at the heat she saw in his eyes again. Her blush intensified. She hightailed it out of the lift without a backward glance.

Alessandro had not long been home with Julian early that evening when the doorbell rang. He opened it to a middle-aged woman and ushered her in. Debbie Woodruff was the tenth applicant for live-in nanny he'd interviewed.

He had no intention of the crèche being a long-term solution for Julian. Yes, it was open 24 hours a day and Julian seemed to like it there, at least when Nat was on anyway, but he'd already been dragged halfway round the world. His son deserved stability. And that was one thing he could give him.

Debbie seemed very nice and was plainly well qualified. Julian was polite, as always, saying please and thank you as Camilla had taught him, eating carefully, playing quietly. But he wasn't enthused. And Alessandro had to admit he wasn't either.

He wasn't sure what he wanted. Someone to love Julian, he guessed. Not for it just to be another job. A pay cheque. What his son needed was a mother.

His mother.

Guilt seized him as he saw Debbie out. The one thing Julian needed the most, and he couldn't give it to him. It was his job. He was the father. He was supposed to provide for his son.

Alessandro entered the lounge room. Julian looked at him but didn't smile or acknowledge him. He sat next to his son and wished he knew how to bridge the gap. Wished his father had been around to be a role model for him, instead of the distant provider. Wished he hadn't let Camilla distance him from his own son.

He looked down at Julian, who was watching television. 'Did you like her?' he asked.

Julian turned and looked at his father. 'She was okay.'

Hardly a glowing endorsement. 'Have you liked any of them?'

Julian shrugged, looking at him with big, solemn eyes.

'Who do you like?' he asked in frustration.

'Nat,' Julian said, and turned back to the TV.

Of course.

Great. Nat, who couldn't mind her own business. Nat, who spoke her mind. Nat of the lift. Nat of the zipper. Nat, who he'd dreamt about every night since they'd met.

Anyone but her.

Alessandro looked down at his son and sighed. Julian wanted Nat. And that was all that mattered.

Nat it was. That he could do.

CHAPTER THREE

ALESSANDRO spotted Nat at the dining room checkout the next day and hurried towards her. He was just in time to hear the waitress say, 'Eight dollars and twenty cents, please.'

He fished out his wallet and handed over a twenty before Nat had even zipped open her purse. 'Take it out of this,' he said.

Nat felt every nerve ending leap at his unexpected appearance. She glanced back at him, her heart doing a funny shimmy in her chest at his sheer masculinity. She frowned, both at her unwanted response and his motivation to pay for her lunch. 'Thanks. I pay my own way,' she said, presenting her own twenty.

The waitress looked from her to Alessandro and Nat couldn't help but notice that when he wanted to, Alessandro Lombardi could indeed pull a hundred-watt smile. His face went from darkly handsome, deeply tortured widower to blatantly sexy, Roman sex god. His curved lips utterly desirable.

After another stifling night with only a fan that seemed to do nothing other than push the hot air around and little sleep, it was especially irksome.

He pushed his money closer. 'Keep the change,' he murmured.

Nat rolled her eyes as the waitress practically swooned as she reached for his crisp orange note. She stuffed hers back into her purse, picked up her tray in disgust and left him to it. Within seconds she could sense him shadowing her.

'Italian women may think it's charming to be taken care of but I don't,' she said, steaming ahead to a table that overlooked the rose gardens St Auburn's was famous for. 'So don't pull your macho rubbish with me.'

Last time she'd let a man pay for her, she'd been sucked in to wasting five years of her life on him.

Alessandro pulled out her chair for her as she angled herself into it and ignored her glare. 'I wanted to talk to you about Julian. I thought the least I could do was buy you lunch while you listened.'

Nat eyed him across the table. She folded her arms. She was damned if the man didn't already know her Achilles heel. She'd spent the morning with Julian and he hadn't seemed any worse than normal. Not that that was much reassurance. 'Is he okay?'

Alessandro's gaze was drawn to the way her crossed arms emphasised the shape of her breasts. She was in crèche clothes today—shorts and T-shirt—and he noticed how her shirt displayed their full, round shape to perfection. He wondered for the hundredth time how they'd feel in his hands. In his mouth.

Damn it!

That wasn't why he was here. He was here for Julian. Not for himself. But it was fair warning that gave him pause. Nat would be very distracting should she be crazy enough to agree to his plan.

'Of course,' he dismissed, annoyed at himself. Seeing her confusion, he hastily added, 'I just wanted to ask you something.'

Nat opened up her packaged egg and lettuce sandwiches and took a bite, intrigued despite herself. 'Ask away.'

If anything, he looked more tired than she'd ever seen him. His hair look more tousled, like he'd been continually running his hands through it, and the furrows in his forehead were more prominent.

'How come you work at both the crèche and the hospital?'

She quirked an eyebrow. Not quite what she'd been expecting. 'You have to ask me that after Ernie?'

He regarded her for a moment. 'So it's a self-preservation strategy?'

'I prefer to call it a happy medium. Too many hospital shifts and I get burnt out. But I miss it if I'm away too long.'

'The best of both worlds?'

She shrugged. 'I like to temper the Ernie days with the Julian days. Both workplaces let me have permanent shifts. No weekends, no night duty. Two days at St Auburn's gives me my hospital hit, keeps my hand in, let's me know I'm alive. Three days at the crèche restores my sanity. It keeps me Zen.'

Alessandro considered her statement. How many years had it been since he'd felt Zen? Definitely not for the last five years at least. Definitely not with her keeping him constantly off balance. 'Do you have child-care qualifications too?'

She narrowed her eyes. Why did this suddenly feel like a job interview? 'I've done my certificate and have a child health qualification.' She cracked open the lid on her can of soft drink and eyed him over the top as she brought it to her mouth and took a swallow. 'Why?'

Alessandro noticed the sheen to her lips and the way her tongue slid between them, lapping at the lingering moisture. He wondered what guava-and-mango-flavoured Nat tasted like.

Inferno! Concentrate, damn it!

He cleared his throat. 'I think I have a solution to your eviction situation.'

Nat felt his gaze on her mouth as if he had actually pressed his lips to hers. Her eyes dropped of their own volition to inspect his. They were generous, soft. Lips made for kissing, made for whispering.

'Oh, yes?' she said cautiously, dragging her attention back to his eyes. Eyes that told her he knew exactly where hers had been.

'You can stay with me.' He watched her pupils dilate and her glance encompass his mouth once again. 'And Julian.'

The canteen noises around them faded as his suggestion stunned her. Live under his roof? A man who, fully clothed, grim faced and utterly inaccessible, made her heart flutter like an epileptic butterfly? What the hell could he do to her in his own place, where the pretence of professionalism didn't exist? Where he'd be all relaxed and homey and...wearing less. What did he wear to bed? She had the feeling he'd be a nothing kind of guy.

'Just until you're unit is built, of course.'

Nat blinked as her mind shied away from images of Alessandro in bed. Naked. 'But...why? I barely know you.'

Alessandro shrugged. 'I have the room, you need a place. And you'd be doing me a favour, helping with Julian. I haven't been able to find a suitable live-in nanny and Julian adores you.'

She frowned. 'You want me to be a...nanny? I already have a job. Two, actually. Which, by the way, I love.'

Alessandro shook his head. 'No. I don't expect you to give up your jobs. Julian can still go to the crèche but he could go and come home with you, which means he wouldn't have such long days there. And he wouldn't have to go on weekends and when I'm called in at night.'

Nat listened to his plan, which sounded very reasonable. So why did it seem so...illicit?

'I'd pay you, of course. And it would be rent free.'

Of course. Nat reeled, her brain scrambling to take in his offer. She looked at him all big and dark and handsome and completely macho Italian with the added grimness that made him heart-breakingly attractive. She didn't know much right at this second but she did know saying yes to Alessandro Lombardi was a very stupid idea.

'No.'

Alessandro's brows drew together. 'You've had another offer?'

Nat contemplated lying. But it really wasn't her way. Already her cheeks were growing warm just formulating a falsehood. 'No.'

He shrugged. 'Then it's settled.'

Nat looked at the haughty set to his jaw and bristled at his arrogant assumptions. 'No.'

'I don't understand. What's the problem?'

The problem was that Alessandro Lombardi was a very attractive man. The mere thought of sharing a living space with him was breathtakingly intimate and already her pulse raced at the thought. She knew enough about herself to know she had a soft heart. And he was still in love with his dead wife. And she wasn't stupid enough to get herself embroiled in that kind of scenario again.

'Ah,' he said as she averted her eyes from him. 'You worry about what people will think? You have my word I have no ulterior motive. I have no…' He searched for the right word, looking her up and down with as much dispassion as he could muster. 'Agenda. Your virtue is safe with me.'

Because it was. His attraction was just physical, a combination of libido and abstinence. Easily tamed.

Nat felt his gaze rake her from head to toe and obviously found her wanting. She felt about as attractive as a bug. One of the really ugly ones. It wasn't something she was used to. 'Gossip does not bother me.'

'Then what?'

She stared at him exasperated. The man was obviously not used to hearing no. 'I don't have to account to you, Alessandro,' she said testily, placing her packaging back on her tray and rising. She wished she had any other reason for turning him down other than his irresistible sex appeal.

But she had nothing. 'I'm sure you're quite unused to hearing the word no. I'm sure you just snap your fingers and women fall all over themselves to do your bidding. But I'm not one of them. The answer is no. Just plain no. No equivocations, no justifications. Just no. Get used to it.'

Alessandro couldn't believe what he was hearing. She was right, once upon a time he had been a finger snapper but that had all ended with Camilla. She turned to leave and he reached across, grabbing her arm. 'Wait. I'm sorry, Nathalie, I didn't mean to be so...'

Nat shivered. She didn't know if it was from his touch or the way her name sighed from his lips like a caress. She turned back. He seemed so perplexed and she felt her anger dissipate as quickly as it had risen. 'Italian?'

Alessandro smiled and dropped his hand. 'You have knowledge of Italian men.'

'I lived in Milano for a year. A long time ago now.'

Ah, that explained her grasp of his language. 'There was a man there?'

Nat gave a wistful smile. She'd lost her virginity in Italy. She'd been eighteen and hopelessly enamoured. 'A boy. It didn't last long. I was a little too...independent for him.'

He nodded. 'So you know we're not very good at asking for things.'

A shard of a memory made her smile broader. 'I don't know. I seemed to remember he was very good at asking for some things.' It had been a heady few months.

Alessandro gave her a grim smile, inordinately jealous at the tilt of her lips and the far-away look in her eyes. 'I meant help. Italian men like to be... men. Yes?'

Nat returned to the present. Yes. She did know that.

'I need help with Julian. We are not…close. Since his mother died…it's been difficult. He doesn't let me in…he's very unhappy.'

Nat swallowed at the raw ache in his voice. It clawed at her soft spot. 'His mother just died, Alessandro. He's grieving, just like you. He's allowed to be unhappy. There would be something wrong if he wasn't. He needs time.'

Alessandro shut his eyes briefly against the pity he saw in her gaze, her words stabbing into his soul. If only she knew. 'I can't bear to see him like this. He likes you, Nat. He smiles, laughs when he's around you. I miss hearing him laugh.'

Nat felt helpless, trapped by eyes that were deep black wells of despair. She'd seen him with his son, maybe had judged him harshly. Too harshly. At least he seemed willing to try. At least he wanted to reach out to Julian.

'Please, Nathalie. If you don't feel you can for you, please do it for Julian.'

His plea was so heartfelt it oozed past every defence she had. She stood staring hopelessly at him, like a rabbit caught in headlights. Knowing she should run like the wind but powerless to do so.

Alessandro saw the compassion in her eyes and knew he'd touched her, could see that he'd struck a chord. 'He needs a woman's touch, Nat. A mother.'

His words stuck in her tightened throat, dragging her out of the compassionate quicksand she'd been sucked into. A mother? She shook her head. He was wrong. Didn't he know that children needed their fathers too? That without their father's love they grew up only half the person they could be? Always wondering. Always yearning.

Damn it—she'd known them for a fortnight. She didn't owe this man anything. Or his little boy. They weren't her responsibility. He wanted to take the easy way out? Use her so he could remain emotionally distant? So he didn't have to try? A substitute mother? He wanted her to be his enabler? She wouldn't. Julian needed his father, just as she had needed hers, and she would not let Alessandro shirk his duties as her father had shirked his.

He had to find a way through this himself. A way to connect with his son. One day he would thank her for it.

She took a deep breath, gathering her courage, breaking away from the spell he'd woven with his beautiful accent and his tragic gaze. 'Children need their fathers too.'

And she turned and walked away, not looking back. She had to protect herself. Alessandro and Julian were a delightful package, right up her bleeding-heart alley. Too easy to fall for.

She'd barely recovered from her last relationship. A man who had claimed to love her yet all the while had still been entangled with his ex-wife. She knew how vulnerable her heart was and she'd be stupid to repeat that mistake again.

So she didn't turn back, even though she could feel his gaze boring a hole between her shoulder blades. Even though her marshmallow centre blazed hot and gooey, berating her for her callousness, urging her to turn around.

It was time to protect herself for a change. Long past time.

Alessandro was more aware of her than he'd ever been when he picked Julian up from the crèche at five that afternoon. It was one of the first days he'd managed to get away on time and Nat was still there. In fact, Julian and Nat were sitting at a table doing a jigsaw puzzle.

It was hard to look at her and know that he had laid himself bare to her, taken a leap of faith, and been rejected. He supposed he was as proud as the next man, maybe prouder. He certainly didn't make a habit of asking anyone for help. He certainly wouldn't again.

He strode towards them, stopping a few feet away. 'Come, Julian, it's time to go.'

Nat's gaze travelled all the way up to the forbidding planes of Alessandro's regal face, etched with lines of tiredness, his beautiful mouth a bleak line. He barely acknowledged her, barely acknowledged his son. He obviously hadn't taken her rejection well.

But she had no intention of letting him take his disappointment out on her or his son. She climbed out of the low kiddy chair and stood. 'Julian, matey, why don't you go and get the picture you drew for your papa today?'

He nodded a silent assent and she watched his unhurried pace as he made his way, slump-shouldered, to his open wooden locker. No welcoming embrace for his father, no jubilant tearing around at the thought of going home. She glanced at Alessandro and caught him also tracking his son's movements.

'He drew a picture especially for you,' she murmured.

Julian hadn't seemed overly excited when she'd suggested that he draw a picture of Papa at work but, then, excited just wasn't a state he ever seemed to inhabit. But he'd attacked the picture with vigour and had spent a long time getting it right, choosing the colours carefully, brightening up the background. And when he'd showed it to her she could see pride and accomplishment in his dark little eyes, so like the ones in front of her.

Alessandro pulled his gaze back to her. 'That's nice.'

Nat cringed at the politeness of his tone but refused to be swayed. She was offering him a chance to bridge the gap with his son. 'You want to know how to connect, Alessandro?' She kept her voice low. 'It's not that hard. Smile at him, touch him, praise him. Show some affection.'

Alessandro felt each suggestion slice into him. If only it was that simple. Camilla was dead because of him. Could any amount of affection make up for that? How could Julian ever forgive him? He clenched his jaw, refusing to comment. Nat could not possibly understand what they'd been through.

He was conscious of her beside him—silent, judgemental—as Julian made his way back to them. He stopped in front of them and held out the picture. Alessandro took it. He didn't want to, he wanted to throw it aside and sweep the boy into his arms, but the memory of Julian's stiff little stance from months ago still clawed at his gut. He couldn't bear two rejections in one day.

Alessandro's gaze went instead to the picture. It was done in crayon. The background was red and purple and quite cheery. The sun shone in one corner and there were trees with possums. The detail was remarkable.

He was in the foreground, nothing more than a stick figure with a stethoscope around his neck, his mouth a grim slash in his otherwise nondescript face. An adult, maybe Nathalie, had written across the bottom in neat teacher handwriting— *'My papa is a doctor. He works very hard.'*

Alessandro gripped the page hard. *That was it?*

Nat was too busy watching Julian to notice the play of emotions across Alessandro's face or the way the paper tore slightly beneath the vice-like grip of his fingers. The little boy's expression was heart-breaking. He was looking up at his father with such hope, his face full of anticipation.

'That's wonderful, Julian,' Alessandro forced out through the chokehold around his throat.

As Nat watched, Alessandro patted his son on the head and Julian's face broke into a broad grin, happy for even that tiny crumb of affection. Not that Alessandro noticed, his gaze still firmly fixed to the picture.

She couldn't believe what she was seeing. She suddenly wished she'd let Julian do rock art so she could beat Alessandro around the head with it. What the hell was the matter with him? Couldn't he see his kid was crying out for love, dying to be swept up and showered in his father's adoration?

It was like her childhood all over again. Once her father had moved on to his new family it hadn't seemed to matter what she'd done, he'd never seemed to notice. And it had hurt—man, had it hurt.

Alessandro dragged his attention away from the picture, his heart heavy. 'Come on, Julian. Get your stuff, it's time to go.'

Nat shook her head. That was it. She couldn't stand watching this…farce of a relationship any longer. Alessandro was obviously clueless. Someone had to teach him how to be a father. And regardless of every flashing light blaring at her, regardless of the attraction that simmered between them, she knew she had to be the one.

She just couldn't witness Julian's emotional isolation one second longer. She couldn't bear him to go through what she'd been through. It was like an arrow through her heart.

'Can I move my stuff in on the weekend?' she asked as Julian's lacklustre pace obeyed his father's instructions. 'There isn't much. Most of its in storage.'

Alessandro was wound so tight it took a couple of seconds for her question to penetrate the barbed wire he leashed his thoughts with. His head snapped around. Had he really just heard what he thought he'd heard? Her gaze was open, steady. It took him all of about two seconds to realise she was deadly serious.

Suddenly the tension that had been holding every muscle taut since she'd rejected him earlier, since Camilla had died, since before then even, since their hasty nuptials, relaxed. It was as if she'd taken bulk cutters and hacked through barbed-wire in one fell swoop.

Everything was going to be all right.

Alessandro nodded. 'That would be most suitable.' He delved into his pocket and handed her a card. 'My number.'

Nat took it hesitantly. For someone who had just got precisely what he'd wanted, she couldn't tell the damn difference. His gaze was carefully masked but she saw the flare in his pupils at the same time she felt a corresponding thrum in her blood as their fingers brushed.

The intensity frightened the hell out of her. 'This is purely business,' she said, lowering her voice. 'Nothing but convenience.'

Alessandro didn't have to ask her to explain. He got the subtext loud and clear. Her husky voice, the slight tremble in her finger tips, the brief widening of her eyes. He knew she was as tuned into their vibe as he was. He bowed slightly. 'Of course.'

He opened his mouth to elaborate further, to assure her, as he had that morning, that her virtue was safe, but Julian joined them and Alessandro nodded at her briefly, said, 'Until tomorrow,' and bade her goodbye.

Nat looked at the card, the pads of her fingers still burning, and wondered what the hell she's got herself into.

Nat pushed the doorbell to the enormous house on a Saturday morning that was already proving to be another scorcher. Her hair fluttered as a warm breeze whipped through the shady portico. She felt jittery but forced herself to concentrate on the wind's caress.

The door flung open and Julian stood there, his curls bouncing slightly as his body trembled with what she could only describe as excitement. Or the nearest thing she'd ever seen in this little boy.

'Nat!' he exclaimed. His dark eyes, so like his father's, literally sparkled as he shifted from foot to foot. 'Papa told me this morning you're coming to live here.'

Nat couldn't help be infected by his barely suppressed enthusiasm. 'Just until my house is finished, matey.'

He grabbed her hand and dragged her inside. 'I hope it never finishes,' he declared.

'Gee, thanks.' Nat laughed as a cloud of cool air enveloped her, instantly dispelling the heat and stroking her exposed arms and legs with icy fingers. She looked up and saw the recessed vent in the ceiling. Ducted air-conditioning. She closed her eyes against the pleasure.

Bliss—instant bliss.

Her eyes fluttered open as Julian again tugged at her hand and she looked around at the large entrance area dominated by white walls, white tiles, white carpet and a large white staircase. She could see boxes left and right in her peripheral vision.

'Come on. I'll show you my room. You're right next door.'

'Julian.'

Julian dropped her hand as Nat glanced up to find Alessandro lounging in a doorway directly to her left, a mug in hand. He was wearing a snug white T-shirt that emphasised the rich golden colour of his skin and every muscle in his chest. His trendy khaki cargo-style shorts rode low on his hips. His feet were bare.

The man had a rumpled look about him, his hair tousled, his jaw unshaven. He looked like he hadn't slept very much and that she could relate to. She'd been awake half the night regretting her decision.

He held her gaze through thick dark lashes and she felt a rush of warmth to places that not even the air-conditioning could cool down.

'Don't crowd Nathalie.'

She opened her mouth to tell him not to call her that. She couldn't live under his roof if he was going to caress her name with his lips like that every time he addressed her. But she saw

Julian's excitement ebb and decided to drop it. For now.

'I would love to see your room. Then I have a surprise for you.'

Julian smiled at her and grabbed her hand again, pulling her towards the ugly monolith that passed as a staircase. She could feel Alessandro's eyes on her as they ascended and forced herself to walk, not run.

Alessandro tracked her path up. She was wearing her standard attire of shorts and T-shirt. Neither were particularly risqué. The mocha shorts came to mid-thigh, the T-shirt was neither low cut or excessively clingy. But there was something about the sway of her hips and the bob of her ponytail that tightened his groin.

Hell. He pushed off the wall and headed straight for the coffee pot.

Nat couldn't believe the clinical waste-land Julian and Alessandro lived in. It was all white—everywhere she looked—and littered with unpacked boxes. Most of the five upstairs bedrooms, two lounge areas and what she pre-sumed was a study were practically bare—except for a few essential pieces of furniture and, of course, the ever-present boxes.

Julian's room wasn't much better, with a bed, a

bedside table with a lamp and a couple of books spread on the floor. There was no colour, no bright quilt or curtains. In fact, there hadn't even been any curtains hung at all. Which made the white of the room even starker as the bright sunlight pushed through the glass.

Maybe Alessandro's wife had been one of those minimalist freaks?

She must have betrayed her feelings because Julian said, 'We haven't got round to unpacking yet. Papa's been very busy.'

Nat's heart nearly broke at the defensive tone and his worried frown. She gave him a bright smile. 'That's okay. I'm here now. I can help with that stuff.'

Julian brightened. 'Your room is next door.'

They went in and she plastered a huge smile on her face as Julian looked at her for any signs of dislike. The room, like Julian's, had a bed and a bedside table. No curtains. But it did have a vent in the middle of the ceiling and it was blissfully cool. 'It's perfect,' she said.

They were walking out when Julian stopped in the hallway and turned to face the end. 'That's Papa's room.'

He pointed to the closed door like it was a forbidden kingdom. Nat bit back her disapproval.

Man, Alessandro was clueless. A far-away room dominated by a closed door? What the hell did he think his son, his four-year-old son, would read into that?

She really did have her work cut out for her.

Nat gave his shoulder a squeeze. 'Want that surprise now?'

Julian looked up at her and nodded enthusiastically, a wide grin firmly in place. She smiled back at him and they made their way downstairs.

'Wait here, it's in the car.' Nat injected a conspiratorial note into her voice.

She was back at the door in a minute—thankfully. The heat seemed even worse after the cool ecstasy of Alessandro's house. She stuck her head round. Julian was waiting there, anticipation lighting his dark features.

'Shut your eyes,' she requested. 'Hold out your hands.' Julian obeyed instantly. 'No peeking,' Nat warned as she adjusted the package in her arms and passed it gently into Julian's waiting arms.

Julian eyes flew open. 'A cat.'

He looked at Nat with utter wonder and squeezed the animal close, rubbing his face into her soft fur. Flo purred appreciatively. In his excitement he even forgot about the weird stiltedness between him and his father and called out to him.

'Papa, Papa, look, a cat. Nat has brought her cat.'

Alessandro appeared in the same doorway as before. Great. A cat. He regarded it warily. Pinocchio had been Camilla's cat and had positively hated him.

'You didn't say anything about a cat,' he murmured, keeping it low for his son's benefit. Not that it mattered. Julian was totally preoccupied by the ball of fur purring like an engine in his arms.

Nat raised an eyebrow at his disapproving frown. 'You're allergic?'

'No.'

Ah. 'If the cat goes, I go.'

Alessandro sighed. He believed her. And how could he deny his son the obvious pleasure? 'The cat's fine. Just keep it out of my room.'

Nat didn't think that would be much of a problem. Flo wasn't one for wasting her time on people who didn't care for her. Especially not when there was a little boy who was obviously going to dote on her.

They watched him for a few moments. 'I trust your room is to your liking?' Alessandro enquired.

To her liking? That was a bit optimistic. 'It's fine. Thank you.'

Alessandro had heard the word *fine* enough in his marriage to know that coming from a woman's lips it didn't always mean fine. *'Problemo?'*

Nat hesitated. But, hell—she had to live here. 'Is there a reason for all the white?'

Alessandro frowned. He looked around. He supposed it was a bit stark. 'No. There's plenty of colourful things—paintings, rugs and so on in the boxes. I just haven't had a chance to unpack yet. This is the first weekend I've had at home since I started at St Auburn's.'

'So you won't object to me adding a bit of… colour, then? I can unpack the boxes if you like.'

'I don't expect you to do that,' he dismissed.

She shrugged. 'It's the least I can do for free rent.' And it wasn't good for Julian to live in such a cold space, devoid of warmth.

He looked at his son, still talking to the cat like a new best friend. 'You're here for Julian, not to be a housekeeper.'

She shot him a pained expression. 'Alessandro, if I have to live in this white palace for even a day, I'm going to go snow blind. Please let me do this.'

Alessandro gave her a grudging smile. Funny

how he hadn't really noticed it until she'd pointed it out. 'As you wish.'

Frankly, if she could make Julian this happy in just a few minutes she could paint rainbows all over the house and sprinkle it with glitter.

CHAPTER FOUR

ALESSANDRO and Julian helped her carry her meagre belongings up from the car. Alessandro withdrew the minute the job was done and she had to admit to being relieved. His presence in her room was too…dominant and she found herself questioning her sanity—yet again.

Julian hovered while she unpacked, leaping at the chance to help her distribute her bits and pieces around the room. Then Flo entered the room and he sat on the floor with the cat nestled in his lap, happy to just observe as he petted the purring animal.

A lava lamp brightened things up considerably in the stark room, as did the orange and russet bedding. Her Turkish rug covered most of the hideous white carpet and Impressionists prints along with her much-loved Venetian masks added colour to the walls. Finally she looped some rich purple gauzy fabric she'd bought in China along the curtain rod, letting it drape haphazardly over the bare window.

She stood back and admired her work. Not bad for an hour's work. At least the room no longer looked like the inside of an igloo.

'What do you reckon?' she asked Julian.

Julian beamed at her, raising Flo to his face and stroking his chin along the top of her soft head. 'It's…beautiful,' he sighed.

Nat laughed. The awe in his voice was priceless. 'Do you think you could do this to my room? Make it like my old one? Before Mummy died?'

Nat felt her heart lurch in her chest at his matter-of-fact words. She scanned his face for signs of distress or grief but found none. Instead, he was looking at her as if she were Mary Poppins and had done it all with a snap of her fingers.

'Sure,' she replied. 'We'll go through the boxes tomorrow and see if we can find all your stuff.'

Nat heard Flo's half-hearted protesting miaow as Julian bounced on his haunches and squeezed her a little too tight. His eyes sparkled and he looked like a normal excited four-year-old.

And she knew in an instant that coming to live under Alessandro's roof had been the right thing.

'Right. Well. I'm starving.' She looked at the slim rose-gold watch that adorned her wrist. Midday. She saw Julian yawn in her peripheral vision and his eyes drift shut briefly as he continued to rub his chin against Flo's head. They'd been having such fun she'd forgotten he was only four and still needed his afternoon sleep.

She realised he would need lunch before going down for his nap. 'Boy, look at the time! Let's get something to eat.'

Julian followed her down the stairs, Flo bundled up in his arms, purring loudly as she wallowed in cat heaven. He led her to the kitchen and Nat braced herself to face Alessandro again. He was working on a laptop at the dining table, which was through an archway to the right off the massive gourmet kitchen gleaming in all its stainless-steel and white-tiled glory.

Alessandro looked up from the recent on-line health alerts from the Australian government concerning the spread of the deadly swamp flu which, due to international travel, could easily be on Australia's shores before they knew it. If he was going to be treating cases of it in his emergency department, he wanted to be forearmed.

Julian was smiling and chatting away and Nat's

cheeks were all pink as she conversed with Julian. 'I trust you've settled in?'

Nat nodded, her gaze settling on his broad shoulders. 'Yes, thank you. Julian and I are going to attack his room tomorrow.'

Alessandro nodded. 'As you wish. I'll locate his boxes and take them up there in the morning.'

'Thank you.'

His gaze held hers, boring into her, like he already knew her, and she suddenly felt out of breath. A lock of hair fell across his forehead and her fingers tingled with the desire to push it back. She could actually see herself doing it in some weird slow-motion flash. Except he didn't have a shirt on. And neither did she.

Nat dragged her gaze away and nervously looked around for something to do. Anything. The stainless-steel fridge was right there and she reached for the door with relish. 'I was just going to make some lunch for Julian and I before he goes down for his nap.'

She stared in the fridge unseeingly for a moment while her pulse settled and her knickers unknotted. 'Shall I make you something as well?' she twittered.

'There's not a whole lot there, I'm afraid. I really need to do a proper shop.'

Nat blinked as the contents, or lack of them, slowly came in to focus. She blinked again. *Now, that was the understatement of the year.* She turned to him. 'What have you guys been living on?'

Alessandro shrugged. He hated shopping. Camilla had always taken care of that. Nothing had been right since she'd gone. 'I usually just pick up a few bits and pieces after work every second day or so.'

Nat pursed her lips. 'Hmmm.' She shut the fridge and glanced briefly at Alessandro. She located the pantry and found it similarly devoid of food. It was obvious they'd just been living from day to day. Was the man totally clueless? Didn't Alessandro know that kids needed a sense of permanency, long-term planning to feel secure? Especially ones whose whole lives had just fallen apart?

'Looks like we go shopping after your nap.'

Julian beamed. 'Can I ride in the trolley? Mummy used to let me ride in the trolley.'

She glanced at Alessandro and saw him visibly pale, his face possibly the grimmest she'd seen yet. She supposed he only used a basket to shop for his bits and pieces and that would seem rather boring to a four-year-old.

Her heart ached anew for both of them. Julian was too young to understand the things that his father was struggling with. 'Yes, you can ride in the trolley. Maybe Papa would like to come with us?'

Nat watched as both father and son tensed. Julian turned hopeful eyes on hers before he looked away, rubbing his chin along Flo's head, and she had to stop herself from going to him and pulling him close.

Alessandro watched in despair as his son fell silent and his little shoulders stiffened. He'd hoped if he didn't push, if he gave his son room and space, that Julian would turn to him eventually but hearing the word *Mummy* fall from his lips had been like a knife plunging deep into his gut and twisting mercilessly. Maybe his son would never let him closer? Maybe Julian also blamed him for Camilla's death?

'I have these journals to catch up on,' Alessandro said, turning back to his lap-top.

Nat stared at two downcast heads. So alike but so disconnected from each other. For a second she felt helpless, but not for long. These two needed intervention and it seemed the universe had decreed she was the one to do it. And she wanted Julian to be close to his father. She wanted to give the little boy the gift of the father-child relationship. She didn't want Julian growing up feeling somehow not whole, as she had. She would never wish those feelings of isolation on anyone, never mind a small child.

But it was plain neither of them were going to make it easy. *She sure had her work cut out for her.*

Alessandro followed the sound of chatter and his nose into the kitchen around five o'clock. The smell of garlic and basil, the aromas of his childhood, and Julian's laughter drew him and he was powerless to resist.

Nat and Julian were cooking. Julian was sitting on the bench next to the cook top, a large metal spoon in hand, stirring something in a saucepan as he fired a hundred questions at Nat. He could see the backs of her long legs, the outline of one very cute derrière and the swish of her ponytail as she chopped and talked and dipped her finger into the saucepan, savouring the taste.

'More salt, Julian.'

Alessandro watched as Julian picked up the salt grinder and handled it as well as a four-year-old could be expected to. He was concentrating hard, his little pink tongue caught between his teeth. It was awkward and he dropped it. Nat was quick, though, and saved it from landing in the pot.

'That's fabulous, Juliano.'

It was on the tip of his tongue to reprimand her for using the Italian form of his name. Despite Camilla insisting it appear on his birth certificate, she actually hated it and had insisted their son be called the anglicised version. But right now he couldn't deny how good it was to hear his son's name being pronounced in the way of his ancestors.

And Julian was smiling at her, swinging his legs as they dangled over the edge of the counter. He was enjoying himself and Alessandro didn't have the heart to spoil that.

'Something smells good.'

Nat faltered as he announced his unexpected presence. She felt every molecule in her body stand to attention. Her nipples jutted against the lacy fabric of her bra, as hard as bullets. Julian's chatter ceased instantly and she noticed his legs stopped swinging in her peripheral vision.

Alessandro noticed it too but steadfastly ignored it as he pushed into the kitchen. 'What are you cooking, Julian?' he asked.

Julian shrugged. 'Spaghetti. The proper stuff. From Milano.'

Alessandro's heart nearly stopped at the perfect way Julian pronounced Milan. He'd always hoped any child of his would be bilingual but Camilla had been adamant.

'Ah.' Alessandro kept his tone light. 'The proper stuff tastes best.'

Camilla hadn't been much of a cook. She'd normally bought pre-prepared food from exclusive delicatessens or supermarkets. Julian had certainly been the best-fed toddler in London, with gourmet treasures bestowed on him every day. When they'd entertained it had always been catered.

But not only had Nat filled his fridge and his pantry and their lives in just half a day but she'd also filled his kitchen with incredible aromas. His stomach growled and he absently realised he was hungry. He couldn't remember the last time he'd eaten for any other reason than as fuel to keep his body going.

When he'd given her his card to go shopping that afternoon he'd imagined she'd buy enough food to get them through the week, but she'd gone way beyond that. He'd helped them unpack and had been amazed at the items she'd considered necessities.

She'd apologised profusely for the amount she'd

spent. He had shrugged it away—money wasn't any impediment for him. Besides, when you'd lost all that he'd lost, it truly meant nothing.

Nat felt rather than saw Alessandro lounge a hip against the bench not far from her. She could also sense that the lovely homey atmosphere from a minute ago had vanished. Julian was tense and she couldn't bear to see a four-year-old so… stiff.

Flo chose that moment to rub against her legs and miaow loudly. *Bless her!* 'Julian, sweetie, would you like to feed Flo?'

Julian brightened. 'Could I?'

'Of course. You know where her bowl is in the laundry and you know where the little sachets of food we bought for her today are. Maybe your papa could help you open one and he could show you how to feed her?'

Nat glanced at Alessandro, praying he'd take the bait. The long journey back to each other had to start with one step.

Alessandro considered her for a moment. Tendrils of hair had escaped her ponytail and framed her face in almost angelic frothery. 'Good idea,' he said, holding her gaze for a moment longer before skirting her and approaching his son. He grabbed an unprotesting Julian under the arms and swung him down to the floor.

'Where's this food, then, Julian?'

Nat kept stirring, not daring to turn around or interfere in any way. Their conversation was hardly natural—in fact, it was so stilted she wanted to cry—but they had to start somewhere. She was relieved though when Julian called Flo and they both left the kitchen. Her shoulders were aching and she slumped a little as the tension left the room and headed to the laundry.

Five minutes later, though, he was back. He didn't have to say a word, she could just feel the hairs of her nape standing to attention. She turned and saw him watching her from the doorway, all dark and brooding, his shadowed gaze heavy against her chest. 'That was quick,' she murmured, turning back to the spaghetti.

'He seemed much more interested in the cat.'

She stirred the sauce. 'That will fade. Give him time.'

Alessandro approached. This was a great angle but he preferred her front. Her open gaze, her perfect mouth. He turned as he reached the bench so his backside leant against it, facing in the opposite direction from her. 'It smells great.'

'Thank you. I figured I couldn't go too far wrong in this house with some pasta and sauce.'

Alessandro allowed a ghost of a smile settle on his lips. He turned so his hip nudged the bench and he was on his side, facing her. 'May I?'

Nat nodded. She stepped back a pace as Alessandro quickly dipped his finger in the sauce. She watched fascinated as it disappeared past his lips, his mouth slowly revealing a totally clean finger.

Damn. It was good. Almost as good as her dilated pupils as her eyes had followed his actions. 'Hmm,' he murmured, licking his lips to savour the residue as he held her gaze. 'You've done this before.'

Nat took a second to pull her body back into line but her voice was still annoyingly husky. 'My host mother in Milano taught me her secret family recipe for Napolitano sauce.'

Ah. Definitely the aromas of his childhood. 'You don't have to cook, you know. Or clean. Or unpack boxes.'

Pleased to be back on firmer ground, she nodded. 'I know. But I enjoy it. It's not much fun cooking for one. I usually don't bother, I'm afraid.'

In truth she missed cooking. And all the other

homey things about being a couple. She'd loved cooking for Rob, they'd loved cooking together. It felt good to be doing it again. Even if it this wasn't any kind of cosy, lovey-dovey relationship.

His gaze on hers was intense and rather unnerving in his grim-faced way. She broke their connection, looking down into the saucepan and giving it another stir. 'I still think it's missing something,' she muttered as she tried to collect herself, blunt herself to his wounded charm.

She dipped the spoon in, blew on it out of habit and brought it to her lips, sipping the rich sauce and not tasting it at all. His eyes were still on her and he was making her nervous. Her hand trembled and the spoon tilted, spilling some of the lukewarm sauce down her chest. It landed on the soft swell of cleavage just visible above the v of her neckline.

Her eyes flew to his, startled by the occurrence. His gaze had already sought it out, tracking the slow trek of the sauce as it unhurriedly made its way south. He licked his lips, involuntarily, she thought as his heated look enveloped her in a raging stupor.

All she could do was watch as he openly stared. Her nipples were the only things moving, scrunching as his hot gaze lapped fire at her skin.

Alessandro could no more have ignored the dictates of his body than flown to the moon. He wanted to taste it, taste her, so badly he couldn't think of anything else. 'I'm good with ingredients. Let me try.'

His voice was like sludge oozing over her and she didn't stop him, just shut her eyes as his head lowered and his mouth closed over the swell of her breast as his tongue lapped at the sauce.

Someone groaned. Was it her? Or him? Looking down at his dark head, she had an insane urge to bury her fingers in his hair, hold him there. Arch her back. Beg for more.

Alessandro felt a strange spiralling out of control as Nat's ripe flesh almost flowered beneath his tongue as he ran lazy strokes over the tempting swell. She tasted sweet and spicy and very addictive. Elicit. Heady.

'Nat, is it okay if Flo goes outside?'

Alessandro lifted his head as if he'd been zapped with a cattle prod, moving away a few paces as Julian's voice called to them from the other room. What the hell was wrong with him? He had his head in the cleavage of someone he barely knew when his wife hadn't even been dead a year.

Julian's mother.

'Sure it is,' Nat called. She'd spun back to face

the cook top, desperately trying to ignore how her skin still flamed where Alessandro's mouth had been.

Julian entered the kitchen, oblivious to the ragged-breath adults, Flo in his arms. 'She ate up all her fish and milk but I think she wants to play.'

Nat turned to face him, plastering a smile over the confusion storming her body. 'Of course she does. Flo loves the great outdoors.'

Alessandro gripped the bench at her blatantly husky tone. 'Not too long, Julian,' he said tersely, distracted by his stupidity. 'Dinner isn't far away.'

Nat saw the confusion in Julian's eyes at his father's harsh tone and watched as he bit into his bottom lip. 'It's okay,' she said gently. 'I'll call you when it's ready.'

Julian nodded, looking deflated, and slumped off. She turned to Alessandro to chide him for his reaction. Yes, she understood where it had come from, but Julian was only four. Except he was gone. Nothing but air where he'd been. She looked to the right in time to see the broadness of his shoulders as he strode out the archway and out of reach.

* * *

Nat stayed in the lounge room till late, watching television that night, too keyed up to sleep. Julian had long since gone to bed and Alessandro, who, apart from a brief appearance to help them search for another knife, fork and plate in the mountain of boxes and eat his dinner, had taken his laptop into his equally barren study and not come out.

A light movie was on and Nat had a headache from forcing herself to concentrate on it and not on what had happened in the kitchen earlier. But force herself she did. What had occurred could never occur again. There was no point building castles in the air with a man who was obviously still so messed up over his dead wife that he hadn't even been able to look at her.

No matter how much he stirred her pulse and her senses and every feminine instinct she had. It was time to rely on other instincts—survival instincts.

The movie ended and she reluctantly made her way to bed. Alessandro's door was open at the end of the corridor, she noticed, but doggedly diverted her attention from it. She checked on Juliano, half expecting to find Flo still curled up with him, but the warm spot where the cat had obviously recently been lying was vacant. She pulled up his covers and turned out his lamp.

She wondered into her bedroom, expecting to see Flo stretched out on her bed. But, no, the cat wasn't anywhere in the bedroom. She knew she wasn't downstairs because she'd just come from there.

'Flo?' she whispered into the darkened hallway, sticking her head out of her open doorway. A distant miaow turned her head in the wrong direction and Nat stared down at the partially open end door. She knew without a doubt that Flo was in Alessandro's bedroom.

Keep the cat away from me. That's what he'd said. *Oh, hell!* She'd done enough damage for one day—she needed to get Flo out.

She tiptoed down the hallway. The thick carpet muffled her footsteps perfectly, she just hoped it also stifled the hammering of her heart. She was sure Alessandro was still in his study, so it was just a matter of sneaking in, grabbing Flo then getting the hell out.

As she drew level with the doorway she whispered, 'Flo,' again. The damn cat miaowed contently and Nat thought seriously bad thoughts about her pet for a moment or two. She gingerly poked her head over the threshold. A low lamp threw a small glow around the room but otherwise the room was empty. Flo sat in the middle of Alessandro's bed, cleaning herself on his espresso-coloured bedding.

'Flo,' she whispered, half scandalised, half scared out of her wits. She did not want to be there but she knew Flo well enough to know that she wasn't going to voluntarily leave—not until after she'd groomed herself anyway.

'Flo,' she whispered again, more loudly, moving closer, trembling too much to notice the minimalist quality of the rest of the house carried through to his bedroom, which had equally sparse furnishings. 'Come here—now! Alessandro will not be amused.'

Flo stopped her fur licking momentarily and regarded Nat with half-closed eyes before stretching her leg in the air and cleaning it with long firm kitty strokes from her little pink tongue.

Nat almost screamed in frustration, knowing she was going to have to climb onto Alessandro's enormous bed and retrieve the recalcitrant cat.

She was two paces away from the bed when a door behind and to the left of the bed suddenly opened and a semi-naked Alessandro appeared before her. His hair was wet and the only thing stopping him from being totally naked was one white towel riding low on his lean hips.

She didn't mean to ogle but she also couldn't

look away. The soft lamp bathed his body in a beautiful bronze glow and, backlit by the en suite light, his face looked more dark, more dangerous than ever.

Her mouth dried in an instant. 'Oh…er, sorry. I didn't know you were…Flo came in.' She pointed to the guilty party like a lawyer holding up exhibit A in a courtroom. The guilty party purred loudly into the tense silence. 'I was just trying to…retrieve her.'

Alessandro hadn't had a woman in his bedroom in a long while. And especially one he'd not long licked Napolitano sauce off. She was wearing the same clothes and the memory came back to punch him in the gut. The taste of her skin, the whimper that had gurgled from her throat, her uneven breath.

He stuck his hands on his hips to quell the surge of lust and the urge to do something more…productive with them. Whether she knew it or not, and he suspected she didn't, her gaze on him was frank and he could feel himself reacting under the towel.

They really needed to clear the air—before he totally embarrassed himself. 'I apologise for this afternoon.'

Nat shook her head, trying desperately hard not

to think about that afternoon while he'd stood before her in just a towel. Avoidance was looking good right now.

'I gave you assurances that your virtue would be safe.'

'Don't worry about it,' she dismissed, her voice practically a squeak.

Alessandro shook his head. 'No. I mustn't…I can't…get involved. My wife…I think it best if we just forget it. It…won't happen again.'

He raked his hand through his wet hair, hating how disjointed he sounded. Hating how the possibilities between them could never be explored. She was nodding at him vigorously and he was pleased she understood.

'You have my word, Nathalie.'

And that's where it all fell part for her. He couldn't call her Nathalie and not expect her to melt into a puddle. Not the way he said it—like a sigh, like a whisper from the devil.

A startling urge to cross to him and whip his towel away was so strong she could actually see it in her mind's eye. Thankfully Flo chose that moment to miaow loudly and spring up from her reclining position, rubbing herself against her owner.

Thank god for kids and animals—where would

they have been today without either of them? *Naked on the kitchen floor. Going at it on his bed.*

She blinked.

'Of course. It was just…' She stroked Flo's fur as she cast around for something to say, some syndrome or insanity plea to blame it on. But with him nearly naked before her, her brain wasn't functioning that well.

'Impulsive.' She picked Flo up and squeezed her tight. 'You're right, it won't happen again.' She backed out slowly. 'Sorry,' she said again. 'About the…' She gestured to his nakedness but couldn't bring herself to say the words. 'Anyway…'

And with that rather inarticulate ending, she turned on her heel and fled the room.

CHAPTER FIVE

THE next morning Alessandro and Julian were up when Nat wandered downstairs. She'd heard the muted noise of the television a little while ago but had lain in bed, wide awake, putting off the inevitable. She'd felt hot and restless all night, despite the air-conditioning, images of Alessandro's perfect flat abdomen and the hot lick of his tongue taunting her through elusive layers of sleep.

The very last thing she wanted to do was face him again. But after a while she knew being a coward wasn't the answer either and she hauled herself out of bed, and showered and dressed to face the day.

Alessandro looked up from his bowl of cereal when she entered the kitchen. He was shirtless and his hair was rumpled. He looked tired, his eyes bleary, like he'd slept even less than she had. And yet still he looked better than any man had a right to.

She really, really needed to talk to him about wearing a shirt.

She gave him a bright smile and kept her eyes firmly trained on his chin. 'Where's Julian?'

Alessandro, who'd stopped chewing in mid-mouthful, swallowed. Nat looked fresh and earthy, her hair loose around her shoulders, her cheeks pink. She was wearing a sundress that sat wide on her shoulders with thin straps that tied in bows and a scooped neckline that drew the eye.

He dropped his gaze back to his bowl. 'Watching television.'

Annoyed at his shirtless state, she advanced into the kitchen and headed for the coffee pot. 'Why aren't you in there with him?'

'I asked him if he wanted me to watch with him and he said no.'

Nat shook her head. 'Don't ask next time.' *Hell, it wasn't rocket science.*

Alessandro frowned at her grouchy reply. 'I'm trying not to push him too hard.'

She opened her mouth to tell him that it was okay to push a little in some situations but Julian bustled into the room and she tore her gaze from Alessandro's.

'Nat! Oh, Nat! You're here. You're really still here!'

Julian launched himself at her, throwing his arms around her legs and squashing his cheek against her thigh. She laughed as she hugged his little body to her legs. 'Of course, silly. I can't leave until my house is built!'

She grinned and ruffled his hair, glancing at Alessandro. He was watching them, his face grave and brooding. Her smile slowly disappeared. Was it hard for him to watch Julian being affectionate with another woman? Someone other than his mother? Did it emphasise his loss even more? Did it twist the knife just a little bit deeper?

She peeled Julian off her. 'I'm making toast—do you want some?'

Julian clapped his hands. 'I love toast!'

Nat busied herself with Julian, chatting away as they shoved slice after slice of bread into the toaster. When they were done she carried it over to the central station where Alessandro was apparently reading a journal. She helped Julian climb onto the stool opposite his father and then plonked the loaded plate in the middle. She topped up their coffees and sat down next to Julian.

'Toast,' she said, not quite looking at Alessandro. 'Eat up. We made enough to feed an army.'

Julian giggled and she grinned down at him but all the while she was hyper-aware of Alessandro and she almost sagged against the counter when his long bronzed fingers reached for a slice. She'd felt his gaze, heavy and intense, on her the entire time they'd been at the toaster and it had been unnerving.

Nat wished she knew what he was thinking behind the brooding mask. Was he remembering what had happened in this kitchen only yesterday or her unscheduled visit to his room last night?

If only she knew.

For his part, Alessandro had been trying *not* to think about what would happen if he pulled one of those little bows sitting snugly atop her shoulders. How easy would it be? Just reach out and tug. Would her whole dress just slide off?

Sitting opposite him, the bows in his direct line of vision taunted him even further. He wasn't following the conversation and was surprised to find he'd somehow managed to pick up a piece of toast and eat it. He tuned back into the chatter when he became aware that both Julian and Nat were looking at him expectantly.

Well, Nat was anyway. Julian was looking wary and the sparkle in his eyes was gone. 'I'm sorry,' he apologised looking from one to the other. 'I wasn't listening.'

Nat gave him a reproving look. 'I was just assuring Julian you were going to help us with the boxes today. Get his room decked out.'

Alessandro looked at Julian. His son didn't seem too enthused by the idea. He was sitting painfully straight in his chair, like a little soldier. 'Ah…well.' He glanced at Nat whose brow had furrowed and then back at his son who seemed to be holding his breath. 'I do have some work to catch up on.'

Nat glanced down at Julian whose bottom lip wobbled and then sharply at Alessandro who was staring down at his journal. She glared at his head but it remained stubbornly downcast. 'Julian, why don't you see if Flo wants a piece of toast?' She scooped up the last cold piece. 'Take it out to the laundry and break it into small pieces.'

Julian squirmed down off the chair enthusiastically and skipped out of the kitchen. Alessandro watched him go.

Nat took a deep breath and gently put down her coffee mug. 'What the hell is wrong with you?' she demanded. 'I just offered you the perfect opportunity to spend time with your son.'

Alessandro gave her a hard look, his eyes chilly. 'He doesn't want me to help. I'm not going to force myself on him.'

Nat got off her stool and stormed over to the coffee pot, pouring herself another. She turned to face him, leaning against the bench, pleased to be far away from his naked chest.

'Sometimes you have to push, Alessandro. He's four. Sometimes children need to be led. You two have to meet in the middle, start doing things together, and this is a perfect place to begin.'

'And what if it has the opposite effect? What if he can't handle what's inside, what if it brings up stuff he was just getting over?'

His eyes were dark and troubled. His frustration and resistance filled the space between them and Nat suddenly understood that this might not be about Julian at all. 'Ah. I understand what this is really about.'

Alessandro snorted. *He was pleased somebody did.* Nothing had made sense for quite a while now. 'Oh, yes?'

'I know that what's in those boxes may be hard to deal with for you. They're your memories. Of your wife and the life you had with her, the one you left behind. But they're his memories too, Alessandro. He's on the other side of the world, far away from everything that's ever been familiar to him. Even his relationship with you is different now. He needs his things around him. And not just in his bedroom but all around him. And he needs to feel like this is home. Not some temporary, half-lived-in dwelling.'

She drew breath for a moment then plunged on again. 'You wanted me to help. You wanted him happy and laughing again. Well, it starts here, Alessandro. And you need to be part of it. You might be surprised what he can handle.'

Alessandro blinked. Maybe she was right. Maybe this was more about him? Maybe the boxes were a bridge too far for him at the moment and he'd been resisting them because of the emotions they were bound to stir? The guilt had been too much to bear as it was.

But if it helped reach Julian…

He stood. 'Okay, sure. That makes sense.'

Nat, who'd open her mouth to strengthen her argument, firmly closed it. He picked up his mug and moved towards her, heading for the sink, his abdominal muscles shifting enticingly with each footfall. She told herself not to look but it was compelling scenery. She gripped the mug hard in case she reached out and touched.

He paused at the sink and drained the contents of his mug. Nat's gaze followed his movements, admiring the glide of his bronzed skin over toned muscle. He placed his mug inside the bowl and it wasn't until he was facing her that she realised he was saying something.

Nat dragged her gaze from the strip of hair that arrowed down from his belly button. 'Huh?'

Alessandro felt desire slam into him right where her eyes had been, as if she'd lapped at his belly button with her tongue. She was looking at him, her eyes slightly glazed, and for a moment they just stared at each other. Her bows taunted him and he curled his fingers into his palms.

'I said when do you want to start?'

Nat's brain grappled with the simple sentence, her annoyance growing. Oh, for crying out aloud, it was just a chest! No reason to lose her mind. Every man had one. Rob had had one. Except, of course, she'd never felt this inexplicable primal swell of lust at the mere sight of Rob. Not even in the beginning.

'Soon. A few minutes.' She pushed away from the bench, the need to get the hell away from him becoming imperative. 'And for God's sake,' she snapped, annoyed at him. And herself. 'Put a shirt on.'

Alessandro stared after her as she stormed out, pleased she and her damn bows were out of sight. Even if his erection wasn't.

* * *

Fifteen minutes later they were all sitting on their haunches in Julian's stark room with one of the two boxes marked *Child* in front of them. Alessandro took a deep breath before taking a Stanley knife to the packing tape.

Nat could see he was nervous. Hell, so was she. After all, Alessandro could be right—what if this whole thing backfired and Julian couldn't handle the memories? What if it upset him too much? If he became inconsolable? But she knew, deep down, that whatever the emotional fallout, father and son needed this.

His biceps drew her gaze, bunching and moving beneath his sleeves as he opened the flaps. She shut her eyes against the temptation—obviously a shirt made little difference to her wandering gaze.

Alessandro opened the box and there, on top, sat Julian's old rabbit.

'George!' Julian snatched up the rather forlorn-looking creature that had obviously seen better days and gave it an enthusiastic hug. 'I missed you, George!'

Watching the reunion, Alessandro felt utterly dreadful. Julian could have had George weeks ago. He hadn't even been aware that the toy had been packed. Or even noticed that Julian had been without him until Nat had prompted him that day at the crèche.

What kind of a father did that make him?

He glanced at Nat and she smiled at him and nodded. 'What else have we got in here?' she prompted.

Julian clung to his rabbit and peered into the box expectantly. They pulled out clothes and toys and books and colourful wall hangings and an exquisite mobile of stars and moons. They were made of brightly coloured glass that formed a whirlpool of colour when the pieces twirled.

'This is beautiful,' Nat gasped as Alessandro lifted it from the box. She could tell it was hand-made, the craftsmanship patently obvious.

'Nonna gave it to me.'

Alessandro looked at his son as Julian reached out and pushed one of the stars with a finger. He smiled. 'That's right.'

His mother had brought it in Murano when she'd been visiting relatives in Venice. He remembered how Julian would lie on his back for ages as a baby in his cot and watch the constellations swing above him in a kaleidoscope of colour.

Julian looked at his father and clutched George tighter. 'Can you hang it above my bed like in London?'

Alessandro expelled a breath he hadn't even realised he'd been holding. It was probably the first time Julian had directly addressed him for anything remotely personal. He nodded. 'Of course.'

They spent a couple of hours putting things to rights in Julian's room, hanging and placing, father and son interacting properly for the first time. And when they'd finished, the room was hardly recognisable. It actually looked like a child lived in it instead of a robot.

There was one thing left in the box and Nat reached for it. It was a box of fish food. She held it up and raised her eyebrows at Alessandro. Julian looked at it and held out his hand for it.

He turned to his father. 'It's Gilbert and Sullivan's food.'

Alessandro looked at the tin. He had bought the fish for Julian's third birthday. Julian had thought he was Superman. Camilla, however, had not been impressed. She certainly hadn't mourned their passing.

'You had fish?' she addressed Julian.

Julian nodded. 'Daddy bought them for my birthday. But they got sick and died.'

'Ah.' Poor kid. His mother had died, his fish had died and he'd had to leave his cat behind.

She waited for tears or withdrawal but he seemed quite matter-of-fact. She glanced at Alessandro. He seemed more affected, the ghost of a smile she'd glimpsed a moment ago gone.

Alessandro's heart thudded in his chest as he contemplated taking the next step forward. 'I can buy you some more,' he offered tentatively.

Julian's face lit up. 'Really?'

'Really.'

Nat felt a lump lodge in her throat at the fragile connection that was being built in just two hours between father and son. Sure, there was a long way to go but it was a start. Alessandro glanced at her and smiled. Actually smiled.

And despite her resolve to keep some distance from him, she grinned back like an idiot.

A couple of days later Nat was working triage when her friend Paige walked through the doors, cradling her listless-looking three-year-old daughter McKenzie. The child looked pale, her limbs mottled.

Paige had been through the wringer in the last few years. McKenzie, a twin, had been born at twenty-seven weeks. She and her twin sister, Daisy, had been very frail and while McKenzie had defied the odds, Daisy had died after a four-month, uphill battle.

It had been a devastating time, compounded by her husband leaving shortly after and McKenzie's chronic health issues. Paige looked tired and pinched around the mouth, her brow furrowed. A far cry from the vibrant woman she'd known back in Perth.

Nat didn't know how she kept going. Not only did she care for her high-needs daughter but she also had to work part time as Arnie, her ratfink ex, refused to pay for anything more than he absolutely had to.

'Paige, what's wrong?' she asked.

'It's McKenzie. I think she's got another chest infection.'

Nat heard the tremor in her friend's voice and ushered her into the privacy of the small triage room. Paige looked as if she was at breaking point and Nat knew her friend, who was running on pride alone, would hate to break down in front of an emergency room full of strangers.

Paige sat in a chair, hugging McKenzie close. She turned beseeching eyes on Nat. 'She's due to have her operation next week, Nat.' She rocked slightly, choking on a sob. 'It took me eighteen months to get her off oxygen and two years to get her to ten kilos and we've had to postpone it three times. Not again, please not again.'

Nat gave Paige's shoulder a squeeze. 'Hey, one step at a time, okay? Let's get her seen to first, huh? I'll just take her temp.'

Paige looked at Nat as she placed the digital thermometer under an unprotesting McKenzie's arm. She gave her friend a watery smile. 'Sorry. Of course. It's just I don't know if I can take much more of this. Thank God for Mum and Dad or I would have gone mad years ago.'

Nat laughed. Paige's parents had been a terrific support after Arnie had abandoned their daughter. 'You're doing fine, Paige. Just fine.'

The thermometer beeped, confirming an alarmingly high temp. 'When did you last give her something for her fever?' Nat asked gently.

'Just before I got in the car,' Paige said.

Nat placed a stethoscope in her ears and listened to McKenzie's chest. It sounded like a symphony orchestra conducted by a tone-deaf conductor inside her chest—wheezing, squeaking and crackling away. She slipped a saturation probe onto McKenzie's toe and the number only read 90 per cent. Paige looked at Nat and worried her bottom lip with her teeth.

'Come on. Come through and I'll get Alessandro to look at her.'

Paige stood. 'I hear he's excellent.'

Nat nodded, avoiding her friend's gaze. 'The very best.'

Nat set Paige up in a cubicle and placed a set of nasal prongs on McKenzie's face. The child, well used to the plastic in her nose and too sick to care, didn't protest. Nat used a low-flow meter to set the oxygen at a trickle. She smiled at Paige, her heart going out to her utterly exhausted friend. 'I'll be right back.'

Nat found Alessandro in the cubicle they used for eye patients. It was set up with a special microscope for high-powered viewing of the eye. She'd triaged Bill Groper fifteen minutes ago after a workplace accident had seen boiling fat splashed into his eye.

Alessandro was leaning forward in his chair, his feet flat on the floor, his legs wide apart to accommodate the low table the microscope rested on. He was staring into the eyepieces, examining his patient's eyes. Bill sat opposite, his chin on the plate, looking in from the other side.

She noticed immediately how the position emphasised the broad expanse of Alessandro's back and how it tapered down to narrow hips.

One strong leg, bent at the knee, was positioned slightly out to the side and the dark fabric of his trousers pulled across his thigh, outlining the slab of muscle she knew, from living in close proximity, defined his upper leg.

She waited for him to finish, knowing that Paige needed time to pull herself together and McKenzie's condition would benefit from the supplemental oxygen.

'You certainly did a good job of it, Bill,' Alessandro murmured. 'Bull's-eye on your cornea.' He pulled away from the eyepieces. He noticed a figure in his peripheral vision and felt his abdominals contract. He didn't have to turn his head to know it was Nat. His body seemed to have a sixth sense when she was around.

'Never do anything by halves, Doc.'

Nat felt a similar awareness and sensed rather than saw his momentary eyelid flicker, which told her he knew she was there. It was probably imperceptible to most, but after a few days of cohabitation and an almost electric awareness of him, she was coming to know all his cues—both obvious and subtle.

Alessandro continued with his patient. 'It's not too bad, though, only superficial by the look of it. Some antibiotic eyedrops should work like a charm.'

Nat lounged against the doorframe and waited. She was used to him ignoring her now anyway. It was a policy they'd both adopted. And as far as it went, it wasn't such a bad idea. There was an attraction there. He knew it. She knew it. It hummed between them like a palpable force, like powerful magnets irresistibly drawn to each other.

But acknowledging it out loud was just plain dumb when neither of them was going to do anything about it. So they were polite. They addressed each other when required and worked together with utter professionalism. In short they carried on as if nothing had ever happened.

Like he'd never licked Napolitano sauce off her chest.

Alessandro stood and Nat spoke. 'Excuse me, Dr Lombardi. I have a patient you need to see.'

Alessandro looked at her fully then and gave her a brief nod before turning back to his patient. He held out his hand and shook Bill's. 'I'll send someone in with some drops for you.'

Nat stepped back from the doorway as Alessandro headed towards her. She could see tension in his shoulders as the looseness with which he'd shaken Bill's hand disappeared and his face drew back into grim lines.

'Three-year-old ex-twenty-seven-weeker. Twin one. Twin two died at four months of age.'

She fell into step beside him, ignoring the lurch of her cells, and launched into the standard summary she'd give any doctor she was handing over to. Here at St Auburn's she was a nursing professional and she would be professional if it killed her. Even if she did want to find the nearest vacant room and tear all his clothes off.

'Chronic neonatal lung disease, oxygen dependent for first two years of life, recurrent chest infections, failure to thrive. I think she's brewing another infection. Febrile. Sats ninety on room air. Bilateral chest crackles. Listless. Cool peripherally and mottled.'

Alessandro nodded as they walked. 'What was her birth weight?'

Nat struggled to keep up with Alessandro's stride, which seemed to lengthen with each footfall. 'Twelve hundred grams.'

'How many days ventilated.'

'Twenty.' The answers to his spitfire questions were well known to her but his emotionless firing of them was irritating.

'Which cube?'

'Eleven,' she said as they drew level with the central nurses' station.

Alessandro nodded. He could smell that flower-garden scent he was becoming so familiar with and, as usual, he had the craziest urge to bury his face in her neck. It didn't seem to matter how fast he walked, he couldn't outrun it. 'Chart?'

She handed the thick file to him but kept hold of it. Alessandro frowned at her. *'Problemo?'*

'Paige is that friend of mine I told you about in the lift that day. She lost a baby, her husband walked out and she's dealing with McKenzie's fragile health. McKenzie's implant operation has been postponed three times in the last year and she's supposed to go in next week for it and that probably won't happen now so Paige is…a little emotional at the moment. Just…I don't know…' She looked at his grim face. 'Smile or something.'

He clenched his jaw and, ignoring her jibe, cut straight to the chase. 'Implant?'

'Sorry,' Nat dismissed, letting go of the chart as she realised she'd left out a vital part of patient history. 'Cochlear implant. McKenzie's profoundly deaf.'

Alessandro looked down at the bulging chart and then back at her. 'Are you coming?'

He didn't wait for an answer and Nat followed him in. The harsh screech of the curtain as he snapped it back didn't bode well and she castigated herself for irritating him just prior to seeing Paige.

Alessandro's gaze encompassed the mother and listless diminutive little girl, hearing aids firmly in place. He gave Paige a gentle smile. She looked utterly exhausted. She looked like he'd felt for the last year and he felt an instant surge of empathy. 'Hello, I'm Alessandro,' he said, and signed it too.

Nat's eyes bugged, as did Paige's. 'Oh. You sign?' she exclaimed.

Alessandro gave a self-deprecating shrug. He had learned the English sign language when he'd moved to London which he believed was similar to what they used here. 'In a fashion.' He smiled. 'I have an aunt in Italy, who's profoundly deaf. I spent a lot of time there as a kid. She was like a second mother to me. My cousin Val, her son, is a renowned cochlear implant surgeon in London.'

He signed as he spoke without giving it conscious thought. Not that McKenzie cared or could probably even understand his mixture of sign language but it was second nature to him when he was in the company of a deaf person.

Nat shook her head, marvelling at the change in Alessandro when he was with a patient. He was great with McKenzie, getting her X-rayed, admitting her for intravenous antibiotics when the films revealed bilateral consolidation and quickly and efficiently placing a drip.

He was especially good with Paige, chatting about sign-language differences and asking her about the scheduled operation. He was like a different man.

Involved. Animated. Connected.

Now, if he could just be more like that at home she could walk out of their lives in a couple of months knowing it had all been worth it.

Even if it meant having to go to bed every night with a fire in her belly and a buzz in her blood that wouldn't quit.

CHAPTER SIX

On Friday Nat was sitting on the quiet mat at crèche with Julian and another boy, Henry. She was trying to encourage a friendship between them. Henry was a nice kid who had been trying to engage Julian for a little while now with not much success.

It wasn't that Julian didn't like Henry—she could tell he did. But he still shied away from other kids, preferring to keep to himself or follow her around. Julian was more than happy to play and talk with Henry as long as she was there as well.

Henry had brought in some photos of his family holiday to New Zealand and they were going through them. There was a beautiful shot of Henry and his mother. He was sitting in her lap, facing the camera. She had her arms crossed across his front, pulling his back in tight to her chest. They were looking at each other, she looking down, Henry looking up and laughing. A massive mountain gave the background some perspective.

Julian took the photo reverently, being careful to only touch the corner as he'd been taught. 'Is that your mummy?'

Julian didn't take his eyes off the photo and the look on his face was heart-breaking. It suddenly struck Nat that there were no photos of Julian's mother anywhere. She'd been so distracted by the starkness of the never-ending white, so snow blind, she hadn't even thought about that.

Goodness, her mother had practically set up a shrine to her father after he'd gone. Despite the fact that he'd deserted them. But she'd been deter-mined to maintain contact, to keep his memory fresh for Nat's sake.

Pity her father hadn't tried as hard.

But there wasn't even a framed picture for Julian to put on his beside table. No family portraits hung on the wall. Come to think of it, not even Alessandro had pictures of the wife he so obvi-ously mourned. Not in his office or his bedroom. It was almost as if she never existed at all.

Was it too painful for him to even look at her? Was his grief still that profound?

And why did the thought depress her so much?

She made up her mind to ask Alessandro about it tonight after Julian went to bed. It seemed to have become her role to ask the hard questions. To be the bad guy. It certainly hadn't taken her long to realise that as much as Alessandro wanted to reach his son he was still floundering and relied heavily on her to facilitate it. They both did. She was like the buffer between them, the referee, and her ruling was final.

Alessandro seemed more than happy for her to take up where his wife had left off. Be some kind of substitute mother to Julian. And she knew that was about his grief more than shirking his duties, that he'd been knocked sideways and was groping in the dark. But she wasn't living with them so Alessandro could hide from his son, to maintain his emotional distance.

She was there until her unit was built and in the meantime she was in Julian's corner. He was a four-year-old child and, God knew, he needed someone in his corner.

Surely there were pictures somewhere? Even one? Alessandro might find it too painful to contemplate but watching Julian now it was obvious he yearned for that connection. If he was to ever recover from his tragic loss, he needed to be able to openly grieve and he needed his mother's life, her existence, to be acknowledged.

* * *

'And next Grandma Poss and Hush went to—'

'Hobart!'

Alessandro chuckled. 'For?' he prompted as he turned the page.

'Lamingtons!'

Julian just couldn't seem to get enough of this damn book—it was their second time through tonight. He seemed to forget everything as the story unfolded. About Camilla. And being dragged halfway across the world. And the stiltedness of their relationship.

At the moment Alessandro was propped against the head of his son's bed, his legs stretched out in front, his son cuddled into his side, Julian's curls tickling his chin.

Nat had been right. This was a special time of the day.

But as happy as he was, it was moments like this that the vile sting of regret was at its most potent. He'd been so busy in London, so involved with his career, with making consultant, that he'd let Camilla drive a wedge between him and Julian.

His guilt at entering into the marriage for all the wrong reasons had convinced him his strained relationship with Julian had been his due. Some kind of cosmic payback. But, then, he'd never imagined his son would be motherless and he would have the sole care of his child.

A virtual stranger…

'Nat bought me a lamington yesterday.'

Alessandro absently rubbed his chin against Julian's soft curls, savouring the texture and this time together. Soon the book would end and Julian would become awkward with him again. Three nights ago Nat had insisted that bedtime was a special time and bedtime stories were a father's role and firmly shoved the book at his chest.

Julian had pouted and begged her to do it but she had just smiled at both of them, kissed Julian goodnight and left them to it. And now here they were, both enjoying the night-time ritual.

Enjoying going to another world far away from their own and all its baggage.

'Did she, now?' he said good-humouredly. 'Did it make you invisible?'

Juliano giggled. 'No. But it tasted dee-licious.'

Alessandro smiled to himself as an image of delicious Nat with Napolitano sauce oozing a tempting streak down the swell of her breast rose in his mind. Not what his son had meant but he couldn't think of a better description.

Had a woman ever tasted so sweet?

Not that it mattered. It wouldn't matter if she tasted like fairy floss, cinnamon doughnuts and dark chocolate gelato all rolled in one. He was paying penance and Nat, who'd no doubt been sent by the devil to tempt him, was definitely off limits.

Nat could hear a low murmuring of voices as she collected her pyjamas from beneath her pillow. A high-pitched giggle carried easily, followed by a deeper, richer baritone that seemed to slither into her room on serpent's wings.

She smiled at the baby steps of progress. Demanding that Alessandro be proactive was doing the trick. She tiptoed down the short distance of hallway between her room and Julian's, unable to resist taking a peek. The sight that greeted her was heart-warming. Father and son stretched out on the bed in the way of father and sons the world over.

Alessandro was still in his work clothes. But he'd taken his tie off and loosened the top two buttons of his duck-egg-blue shirt. His feet were still encased in his socks. He looked relaxed for a change. Younger, even. Devoted, certainly.

Also hot, sexy and virile. What was it about

seeing a big man with a small child that was irresistibly attractive?

Julian's little body was curled up, knees to
chest, snuggled into Alessandro's side. His small
hand rested on his father's shirt, making it seem
positively diminutive against the sheer size of
Alessandro's chest. He was looking at his father
as he read the story like he could leap tall build-
ings in a single bound.

No one watching this scene would guess at the
strange relationship that had existed between the
two of them. The stilted politeness, their mechani-
cal interactions, the distance. Right now it was as
it should be and her foolish soft heart practically
over flowed with joy.

She tiptoed away, a small smile curving her soft
mouth, knowing that things were looking up and
she was part of it.

An hour later, Nat, her heart thudding in her
chest, knocked on Alessandro's office door. It
wasn't shut, just pulled to, but, still, it was a bar-
rier she didn't feel comfortable breeching without
an invitation. He shut himself away every night
after Julian went to bed. The relaxed man who lay
with his son disappearing the second he walked
out of Julian's room.

His message couldn't have been clearer—back off. Keep out. He'd said they should pretend it had never happened and he was hell bent on leading by example.

She heard his soft '*Entrato*' and hesitated briefly, girding her loins for the forthcoming battle. One thing she'd learned very quickly had been that Alessandro was an intensely private man. She didn't think he'd take too kindly to her entering these particular waters. He didn't talk about his wife, he hadn't even let her name slip. Nat had no way of knowing how he'd react to the photo issue.

But she'd made a commitment to herself that she would raise this with him, for Julian's sake, and she wasn't going to back down. She took a breath and pushed open the door.

He was sitting in his black-leather, Italian-designed swivel chair. His computer was on. Open textbooks cluttered the surface of the desk and the floor around his feet. Piles of medical journals, some open, littered the area as well in some kind of order...she guessed.

The rest of his office was still stark. The walls were bare and the whiteness was harsh in contrast to the cluttered desk area. She made a note to attack those boxes this weekend. Surely

Alessandro wanted familiar things around him too? Maybe he'd appreciate a photo of his wife for his desk?

He'd changed out of his work clothes into his pyjamas. Boxer shorts, the soft clingy kind often seen on models, not the loose, silky ones. They came to mid-thigh and revealed more than they covered. As did a snug-fitting white T-shirt. He'd avoided being 'undressed' around her, for which she was most grateful.

The occasional glimpses she'd caught of him *sans* shirt had been hard enough.

His hair was damp as if he'd not long been out of the shower. A soft lamp spread a glow around the office and settled against the angles of his face, emphasising the richness of his bronze complexion and shadowing his mouth. He looked dark and dangerous and breathtakingly good-looking.

Her very first thought was to turn around and run.

Alessandro raised an eyebrow. 'You wanted something?'

Nat swallowed. His voice was a low purr, like Flo's—on steroids. *God help her, she did.* She wanted him like she'd never wanted a man before. Not even Rob. She shut her eyes against the image of her and him going for it in his big old chair that flashed briefly through her mind.

No! They couldn't do this.

When she opened them again his dark gaze netted her in its web. It was if he knew exactly what she'd been thinking.

Alessandro flattened his bare feet in the carpet so he wouldn't leave the chair and cover the short distance between the two of them and snatch her into his arms. Nat's gaze had licked all over him and become all heat and steam and he suddenly felt like he was sitting in a sauna or a hot spring. He kept his gaze trained on hers despite the compelling tug to let it wander down over her cleavage and further to her long bare legs and feet he could see in his peripheral vision.

Inferno! This was crazy. 'Nat?'

His voice was steely now, pulling Nat back from temptation. 'I wanted to talk to you about…' she swallowed '…something.'

Alessandro's gaze took in her mouth as she talked and her nervous throat bob. The strange urge to stroke a finger down the ridge of her windpipe, place kisses along it, came upon him and he curled his hand around the arm of the chair, anchoring himself. 'Okay. So talk.'

Nat nodded, still uncertain how to go about

asking the question. 'I was wondering if…' He was staring at her mouth and she couldn't process anything. She took a second. Probably best to just say it. 'You had any photos of your wife?'

Alessandro's gaze flicked back to her eyes in an instant. He felt the tension that was never far way come back into the muscles of his neck. 'What for?'

Nat heard the note of foreboding, the no-trespassing inflection in his wary voice. And the urge to flee became an imperative. Her heart beat loud enough that she felt sure that Alessandro must be able to hear it. 'I thought it would be nice for Julian to have a picture of her on his bedside table. Maybe one of them together?'

Alessandro stiffened, an immediate denial rushing to his lips. They'd made real progress this week. He couldn't bear to see Julian return to the practically mute little boy he'd been in those few days and weeks after Camilla's death.

His son was moving on, he didn't want to take him back. 'I think that would make him un-bearably sad again.'

Nat steeled herself to be the bad guy again. 'His mother's dead, Alessandro. He's allowed to be sad.'

Alessandro shook his head. She didn't know how hard it had been. 'It's too awful to watch.'

Nat nearly gave up then and there. The anguish in Alessandro's voice cut her to the quick. But she knew enough child psychology, as should he, to know he wasn't doing his son any favours. 'You can't protect him from that. It's healthy to be sad, to cry, to grieve. You can't fast-forward this bit by pretending she didn't exist.'

Alessandro's head snapped up. 'I'm not doing that,' he denied, ice lacing his voice and turning his obsidian eyes flinty.

Alessandro's fervent denial flared out at her like a striking snake. 'There's not a single photo of her anywhere, Alessandro,' she persisted, keeping her voice even and gentle. 'You loved her. She was the mother of your child. I know it's hard for you to have reminders of her around —'

Alessandro's snort interrupted her. 'You have no idea.'

Nat frowned, surprised at the derision in his voice but ploughed on anyway, not sure she'd ever be brave enough to say it again. 'He's four, Alessandro. You know I'm right. Put aside the father, the husband, for a moment and think like a doctor. Like the good doctor you are. You know

I'm right. You know this is good grief resolution strategy.'

Alessandro cursed her for being right. 'And what if I can't look at her?' he demanded.

How long had it been since he'd looked at Camilla's face? Conjured her up? He'd been trying so hard to banish the years of baggage he'd steadfastly refused to imagine her at all.

Of course, he didn't have to look too far for a reminder. But funnily enough, the physical similarities between Nat and Camilla didn't strike him any more—hadn't since that first meeting. They were two different women in so many ways. Too different to be mistaken as the same one.

Nat swallowed. She felt his pain all the way down to her toes and felt dreadful, pushing. 'I'm not asking you to commission a six-foot mural on one of these god-awful walls. Just a photo for Julian's bedside table. So he knows she existed and she loved him and she's looking over him.'

Alessandro wished it was that easy. Could he look at that photo every time he entered his son's room? Could he look at it and not feel the knife twisting a little deeper?

He looked at Nat's earnest face and sighed. Hadn't she been right about everything else? Hadn't she helped him reach out to his son already? Of course he could do it, if it helped his son mourn.

'There are framed photos,' he sighed. 'A few. In one of the boxes.'

It had been his intention to get around to putting them out. In their house in London, photos of her, of them, as a family had been everywhere. They'd been so hard to look at afterwards. The hypocrisy had been torture. And frankly he'd been enjoying the emotional freedom.

Nat felt her heart sink at both the defeat in his voice and the thought of having to search through the remaining mound of boxes. Whoever the packing company had been, they'd done a lousy job. Most of them were marked miscellaneous so the photos could be anywhere.

But it was a start, a concession. And there was no rush now that Alessandro had consented—they'd find them some time in the next few weekends and with Alessandro on the same page it would be a good avenue to open discussion. And in the meantime they could sound Julian out about the idea.

She noticed how tired he looked and suppressed her natural soppy-female instinct to go to him. She wanted to put her arms around him, hug him, give him a place to rest his head. But she knew it would be a mistake. The urge to comfort might be her motivator but she doubted it would stay that pure for long.

'Thank you. This is the right thing to do, Alessandro.'

Alessandro heard the note of genuine belief in her voice. She stood in his doorway, oozing certainty and confidence. God, he felt so out of his depth sometimes. And yet here she was in her T-shirt and shorts, all perfect and Zen and centred, telling him it was going to be all right.

He wished she'd come nearer. He wanted to put his arms around her, bury his face against her belly. Absorb some of that Zen she had going on. Maybe feel her hand sifting through his hair. 'I hope so,' he murmured.

Nat was almost paralysed by the longing she saw in Alessandro's gaze. Was it desire to connect with his son or just plain old desire?

Desire with a capital D?

His eyes roamed over her and her skin felt like it was on fire. The room had become a furnace, heat roaring between them. She opened her mouth to say something but, as if he knew he'd already given away too much, he swivelled the chair back around to face his desktop monitor.

She stood in the doorway for a few moments,

staring at the back of his chair, trying to catch her breath. This was a good thing. Something happening between them would be dumb—way dumber than Rob. He was doing them a favour.

And one day, she had no doubt, she'd truly appreciate his resolve. But right now a long lonely night stretched endlessly ahead.

Nat woke in the wee small hours to Flo miaowing and nudging her. Rain drummed on the colour bond roof. She wasn't surprised. The day had been humid and a storm had been brewing as she'd climbed into bed. She stroked Flo, lying there for a second just enjoying the noise and luxuriating in being dry and snuggled beneath the covers. But Flo persisted with her nudging and Nat reluctantly got up.

'All right, bossy-boots. I know you like to frolic in the rain, you crazy cat.' She picked up a purring Flo. 'Come on.'

Familiar now with the layout of the house, Nat made her way downstairs in the dark and opened the laundry door for Flo to go out. She watched the cat bound into the rain and grinned. Silly animal—giving up a dry warm bed snuggled into a doting little boy to chase a few raindrops around.

Nat shut the door, knowing Flo would be happy out there for hours. She stopped and grabbed a drink of water in the kitchen and headed back to the stairs. A chink of light from beneath the office door caught her gaze. Good grief! Alessandro was still up?

She knocked lightly on the door and waited for his gruff *'Entrato'* but nothing. She pushed it open slowly, expecting him to swivel around with an annoyed look on his face. Instead, he was bent forward in his chair, head on desk, amidst the clutter of textbooks, his eyes closed.

'Alessandro?' she whispered, approaching carefully. He didn't stir and she stood for a moment just looking down at him. His black hair fell across his forehead, disarmingly innocent, just like Julian's did when he slept.

But the dark growth shadowing his jaw and his softly parted lips were one hundred per cent adult.

It was a shame to wake him—he always looked so tired. In fact, even asleep he looked utterly exhausted. But he'd have a hell of a sore neck in the morning if he stayed like this.

'Alessandro,' she called again as she gave his shoulder a gentle shake.

Alessandro startled, sucking in a breath and

sitting bolt upright as he dragged his body out of the sticky depths of slumber. His hand automatically went to the twinge in his neck as his brain scrambled to get up to speed.

Nat standing in his office. Nat standing really close in his office. Nat wearing some clingy T-shirt dress thingy with no bra standing close in his office.

'I'm sorry,' he murmured, struggling with the urge to drop his gaze to the bounce of her unfettered breasts in his peripheral vision. 'I must have fallen asleep.' He used both hands to rub his neck for fear of where they'd go if they weren't occupied.

He had a red mark on his cheek where it had been stuck to a textbook and Nat had a crazy urge to stroke it. 'What are you doing up so late?' she whispered. She wasn't sure why she was whispering. It just seemed appropriate in the dead of night.

Alessandro shrugged. 'I've been working on St Auburn's readiness for pandemic status should the dreaded swamp flu reach our shores.'

'It's two-thirty in the morning,' she chided. 'The swamp flu can wait. Go to bed. Get some sleep.'

Alessandro let his hands drop. If only if was

that easy. 'I can't sleep,' he murmured. 'I never sleep.'

Nat felt his weariness, his anguish, right down to her toes. He looked totally wretched and her instincts cried out to comfort him. 'Oh, Alessandro,' she whispered.

She didn't give a second thought to moving closer, sliding one hand behind his neck and one into his hair, cradling his head, pulling it against her belly. 'I'm so sorry.'

Alessandro's arms automatically encircled her waist, drawing her closer. He shut his eyes as he leaned into her, his face pressed into her night-shirt. She smelled like soap and rain and flowers. And he wanted her. 'I'm tired. I'm so tired.'

'Shh.' She cradled his head and rocked slightly. 'I know. I know.' Because she did know. She knew what it was like to grieve the end of a relationship. To lose someone close.

He pressed a kiss to her belly and looked up at her. She was so beautiful. Her eyes were shimmering pools of empathy, her skin was glowing and her mouth was beckoning. He wanted to crawl into a nice, big warm bed with her and stay there for ever. 'Nathalie.'

Nat shook her head. She knew that look in his eyes. Knew for damn sure it was reflected in hers.

'Don't call me that.' Her voice shook. She hated how husky it sounded.

He rubbed his chin against her stomach. 'Why? It suits you.'

Her abdominal muscles rippled beneath his stubble as if he had licked them and deeper down other muscles stirred deliciously at the way he'd sighed her name. Her hand drifted down from his hair to his face. She rubbed gently at the red mark on his cheek with the back of her hand. 'Because I like it too much.'

They stared at each other for the longest time. They didn't move. All that could be heard in the small office was the rain on the roof and the staccato rhythm of their breathing. It was Alessandro who made the first move, applying pressure through his arms, bringing her down onto his lap, their heads close. Their lips closer.

Nat didn't protest, mesmerised by his eyes, by the desire that gleamed there. That they could be cold like black ice one moment and warm like sable the next. She wasn't supposed to be here, doing this, but she also knew she was utterly powerless to resist. She could almost feel his mouth on hers, taste it, and she wanted it so badly anticipation hummed through her system.

Alessandro's hand crept up, brushed against her

shoulder and moving along the line of her collar bone until it was cradling her nape, four fingers lodged in her hair, his thumb stroking her jaw. He exerted slight pressure inching her closer. Their mouths nearer.

'*Bello*,' he murmured. He was past caring about restraint and all the reasons why kissing Nat, taking her clothes off and having her right here, right now, was a bad idea. All he knew was that in amongst all the bad things in his life at the moment this felt inextricably right.

That he suddenly felt more awake, more alive than he had in a long time. A very long time.

His hand drifted down to her neckline, coming to rest where the material scooped low on her breasts. She shut her eyes as her nipples responded to the blatant arousal. She watched fascinated as he dropped his head and kissed her not far from where the sauce had landed not even a week ago. His lips practically sizzled against her skin and she arched her back involuntarily.

'Nathalie…'

She barely had a chance to whimper before his mouth brushed against hers. Light. Gentle. A whisper of what was to come. 'Alessandro.' She wasn't sure if it was a warning or an invitation.

But it was definitely surrender.

Her hands snaked around his neck at the same time and their lips met again. Not gentle now. Not light. Deep. Deeper. Open mouths and questing tongues feasting on each other like starving beasts. She could hear his moan and felt its seductive stroke deep inside her before it travelled all the way to her toes.

Her head spun as the kiss spiralled out of control. She broke away for a second, dizzy and out of breath. Alessandro looked at her with a passion not even his hooded eyes could conceal. His lips were moist from her ministrations—full and beckoning.

She'd done that to him. Made this man look at her with eyes that devoured her, that branded her. She should be scared by this level of intensity but, God help her, she wanted more.

Alessandro rubbed his thumb across the soft swollen contours of her mouth. She had him on her lips. Them. And he wanted to be back there. Their mouths joined. To be joined even more intimately. To taste her more intimately. To be inside her. 'You're so sweet,' he whispered.

'So are you,' she murmured, before slamming her mouth back on to his.

He met her ardour, surpassed it. His hands tangled in her hair, holding her captive, making escape impossible. Not that she wanted it. She could feel he was hard for her, his cotton boxers and her position on his lap giving his impressive arousal nowhere to hide.

She squirmed against it, wanting to feel it pressed against her more intimately, not just the back of her thigh. She wanted to touch it, damn it. Without breaking the kiss, she manoeuvred herself until she was straddling his lap, her night-dress riding up her thighs.

Thank God for quality Italian furnishing.

The big leather chair accommodated her most adequately and she wasted no time grinding down against him, seeking the pleasure, the relief she knew he could give her.

He broke off the kiss on a groan, his breath outdrumming the rain. 'Nathalie.' She was beautiful, bits of her blonde hair wisped free from her ponytail and somehow, despite the experienced movements of her hips, she looked down at him with a wide-eyed wonder that could almost border on innocent. 'I want to see all of you.'

Without asking, his hands snagged the hem of her nightdress, lifted it up and dragged it off over her head. She was totally naked apart from a very inadequate scrap of lace. Her breasts fell free and he was mesmerised by them. They were as beautiful as he'd imagined, and God knew he'd imagined them often enough. Full and firm with nipples the colour of mocha.

He brought his hands up from her waist until they were full of her. They felt heavy in his palms and her peaked nipples dragged deliciously across the sensitive skin there. *'Inferno!* I want to taste you.'

And then, with one arm around her back, he swept her close, his mouth latching onto the nearest offering. He sucked hard on her nipple and Nat cried out, clutching his shoulders as her world tilted and spun.

His tongue rasped against her peaked flesh. It lapped and licked and sucked and rolled around the entire elongated peak. And just when he thought she could take it no longer he released her and she almost fell against him. But he steadied her with his arm and opened his mouth over the other one.

'Alessandro!' She wasn't sure if she was begging him to stop or egging him on further—all she knew was she was swirling like an autumn leaf in the wind and they hadn't even got to the main event.

Alessandro released her nipple, satisfied to see

it wet and puckered from his ministrations. 'I want you.'

Three little words. Not the three words most women want to hear but Nat couldn't have cared less. She'd heard those words and they'd been an empty promise. Right now she needed this. Alessandro. A man who wanted her with an intensity she doubted she'd ever known.

But even so. There were some logistics that needed sorting. She battled with her breathing. 'Condoms?' she panted.

Alessandro shook his head. 'Are you on the Pill?'

She nodded. She could feel the ridge of his erection pressing against her and she was desperate to feel it inside. 'Of course. But it's about more than that, Alessandro.'

His arms tightened around her. Damn it. He knew that. 'I've had sex with one woman in the last five years.'

She looked into his eyes, warm like sable still, and saw the yearning and desperation that had got her into this chair in the first place. He wanted her. But he was telling her he was safe and, God help her, she'd die tonight if she had to leave this room unsatisfied. 'Same with me.'

'Good.' Alessandro returned his attention to

her breasts and she grabbed his shoulders as lust slammed into her gut.

Barely thinking straight, she reached down for him, finding him bigger and harder and thicker than even she'd imagined. He moaned into her mouth and she felt a surge of warmth between her thighs as her body prepared to take him.

Alessandro pulled away as she manoeuvred him out of his material prison and her hand finally found bare skin.

'Nathalie...' he groaned, leaning his forehead against her chest. 'I don't think I'll last very long if you touch me like that.' He looked up into her face. 'It's been a long time.'

Nat squeezed his girth, her hand luxuriating in the velvety glove sheathing the core of solid rock. He snatched in a breath and expelled it on another groan and she smiled down at him. 'Good. We can do slow later.'

And she lowered her head, opening her mouth over his, feeling him surge in her palm as his tongue thrust inside her mouth. She felt his hands squeezing her buttocks, dragging her closer, and she rubbed herself against his naked length, aroused beyond all rational thought.

There was no planning now. She was just moving to a rhythm as old as time. She needed to feel him inside her and without conscious control she was lifting over him, pushing the crutch of her knickers to one side, and then his head was nudging her entrance and she didn't even pause before her hips moved instinctively down as his moved instinctively up.

She cried out as he filled her more than she'd ever been filled before. She vaguely heard him calling her name but a pounding in her blood, like jungle drums, was taking over and she moved to their beat.

Alessandro groaned, hearing the drums too, and moved again, pulling her close, one arm still around her back. He kissed her lips, rained kisses down her neck, took a puckered nipple in his mouth, all the time obeying the throb in his blood, the rhythm in his head.

Nat held Alessandro's head to her breast, hanging on for dear life as the beat became a canter and then a gallop. 'Alessandro!' she cried.

Alessandro barely heard her above the tempo pulsing around him. It was inside, thickening his blood, and around them, pressing them closer with invisible hands. His loins moved to its beat, surging and thrusting into her hot, tight core.

Nat felt the drums rise to a crescendo and she

knew she was going over the edge. 'Alessandro, I can't…Oh, God, I can't stop it.'

'Nathalie,' he roared, throwing his head back against the leather headrest, clutching her hips. He thrust one last time as the rhythm peaked and he along with it.

For a moment neither of them moved as the drums crashed to total silence and they both became airborne. And then Nat moaned and bucked, her nails digging into his shoulders as pleasure, so deep, so profound, rained down on her.

And Alessandro joined her, thrusting his hips, pumping up into her, riding the wave of his own orgasm, driven by the echo of the drums still spiking his blood and milked by her wild abandon as she bucked and rode him to completion.

And when it was over she collapsed against him and he gathered her close and he knew without a shadow of a doubt that having Nat Davies come to stay was the best thing he'd ever done.

CHAPTER SEVEN

AFTER not knowing the pleasures of a woman's body for a long time, Alessandro was insatiable. They'd made love another twice that night before Nat had slunk back to her own bedroom. And then every night since. Alessandro would put Julian to bed, read to him and then he would pounce again, no matter where she was. The kitchen, the shower, the laundry, the lounge. A week later there were very few places in the house they hadn't done it.

Thank goodness Julian slept like the dead.

It never crossed Nat's mind to refuse Alessandro. She'd been around long enough to know that the magic they'd made that first time didn't come along very often. And, anyway, her body betrayed her at every single turn. All he had to do was look at her and she practically self-combusted.

Why deny herself this little oasis of pleasure? As long as she took it at face value, remembered it was about two convenient bodies finding a little mutual gratification for a finite period of time, she'd be fine. She was an adult. There was nothing wrong with that.

For once in her life she was making a decision with her head and not her poor, easy heart.

And it felt liberating.

Plus there was something compelling about Alessandro's love-making that was addictive. He was so…driven. Intense, like the rest of him. Desperate, almost. When his body covered hers it felt like he was trying to absorb her into him. He wasn't satisfied with quick and easy and rolling over and going to sleep. They made love for hours each night until sheer exhaustion took over.

And his attention to detail was amazing.

Nat doubted she'd ever been so thoroughly bedded in her life. It was like by reaching for the maximum level of pleasure he was hoping to purge the grief. Not just sideline it. He was still hurting and it was if he'd found the perfect antidote for it—her body. And that was okay too. If her gratification helped him heal, who was she to argue?

And then there was the flow-on effect to Julian. The sex was making Alessandro more relaxed. He didn't seem so grim. He was more…laid-back.

He smiled more. Laughed. And Julian was slowly becoming less serious, less wary in return.

They were careful, of course, to keep their relationship from Julian. Nat was always back in her bed by five a.m. It was hard and getting harder, especially when Alessandro was so warm and vital, his big arm tucked around her waist, his bigger body curled around hers.

And at that hour of the morning he was usually raring to go again with another treacherous seduction muddling her senses.

'Stay longer,' he'd whisper. His accent always seemed more pronounced when he was sleepy and it stroked seductive fingers along her pelvic floor.

Nat would smile as his lips nuzzled her neck, his hands kneaded her breasts and his erection brushed her belly. The temptation to stay was great. 'Julian,' she'd murmur.

'He never wakes before seven, *bella*.'

Which was true, but Nat knew it was best not to be found together. Choosing to snatch these moments with Alessandro was fine—she was an adult. Julian was a boy who dearly needed a mother and who plainly adored her. And that wasn't fair. What did four-year-olds know of adult games? Adult relationships? It wasn't right to confuse him any more when his world had already been turned upside down.

So she dutifully dragged herself out of her lover's bed, out of his possessive male embrace, every morning. And even when he looked up at her with a sexy half-smile and smouldering sable eyes that told her more than words what he wanted to do to her, she still turned away.

But it was getting more and more difficult...

Alessandro had tried to not let their chemistry spill over into their work and for the most part it was successful. She only worked two day shifts a week in the department and usually it was on the triage desk so it was easier to avoid direct contact.

But today, on this crazy, crazy Friday, she'd been allocated to the cubicles and they seemed to have giant magnets attached to their butts. Today it was simply impossible to ignore her and their attraction. Impossible to not be utterly distracted by her.

'Twenty-year-old female, right lower quadrant pain, rebound tenderness, hypertensive, tachycardic, febrile.'

Nat pushed the chart at Alessandro, trying to be brisk and professional in her handover.

Everywhere she'd moved today his incendiary gaze had been on her and she was about ready to combust.

Not to mention the fact that despite his dark trousers, dove-grey shirt and beautiful mauve tie, all she could see was the way he had looked last night on his way back from the bathroom gloriously naked, hands firmly on narrow hips, his arousal on proud display.

Alessandro smiled. He could see the simmer in her gaze and knew exactly where her brain was. 'Which cubicle?'

'Twelve,' she said automatically, a vague part of her still clinging to professionalism while his rough command from last night to 'Open your legs' squirmed through her grey matter.

Nat felt her internal muscles twist firmly in a knot. His broad shoulders bobbed in front of her and she followed blindly, trying to catch her breath.

Alessandro greeted his patient. 'Hi. Ellie? I'm Dr Lombardi.' He held out his hand and the harried young woman shook it briefly, grabbing her side with a grunt as she let go. 'Nat's been telling me you have some pain.'

'Yes,' Ellie agreed. 'The odd niggle the last

day or two but worse this morning. And by the time I got to work it was unbearable.'

Nat watched as his attention turned solely to his patient. He questioned her closely before methodically examining her. Even in significant pain she could see how Ellie responded to Alessandro's calm professionalism. She was scared but somehow he managed to reassure her.

Alessandro returned his gaze to Nat. She was looking at him with admiration and respect and even that went straight to his groin. 'I'll call for a surgical consult. In the meantime I'll write up some morphine and let's draw some blood, Nurse Davies.' He handed back the chart and deliberately let his gaze fall to her mouth.

Nat's lips parted involuntarily as she took the chart. It felt as if he'd physically touched them. She reached for the bed rail and cleared her throat. 'Certainly, Dr Lombardi.'

And then he was gone from the cubicle and she was left staring after him, her lips tingling, her brain scrambled.

'Do you think I can get that morphine now?'

Nat dragged her attention back to her patient. Ellie was grimacing and clutching the sheet tight. 'Oh, sorry, of course. I'll be right back.'

Nat exited the cubicle determined to keep her

mind on the job. 'Imogen,' she called seeing her boss. 'I need you to check some morphine with me.'

Imogen followed her into the room where the narcotics were stored. She inserted the key into the locked metal cupboard as Nat smothered a yawn.

'Are you not sleeping well?' Imogen asked as she reached for the boxes of morphine. 'You yawned all the way through handover this morning and you look like you haven't slept in a week.'

Nat busied herself with writing in the dangerous-drugs register to hide the sudden rise of heat to her cheeks. She was sleeping very well indeed. When she and Alessandro finally succumbed, they slept the deep sleep of the sexually sated. It just so happened that it only amounted to a few hours each night.

It had certainly been well after three last night before they'd worn themselves out. 'I'm fine,' she murmured.

Imogen removed a morphine ampoule and they counted the remainder. Nat drew up the injection as Imogen signed the register then they left the room together and entered cubicle twelve.

Imogen smiled at the patient. 'Can I have your

full name, date of birth and any allergies, please?' she asked.

Ellie prattled off the requested information as Imgoen and Nat checked it against her patient number in her chart and on the medication form. Satisfied they had the right patient, Imogen departed, leaving Nat to administer the needle.

'Thigh or bottom?' she asked.

'Oh, God, I don't care,' Ellie groaned. 'You can stick it in my eyeball as long as the damn pain goes away.'

Nat smothered a smile. 'I think your thigh will be easier,' she said, exposing her patient's leg. 'You don't have to move.' Nat prepped the area with an alcohol swab and delivered the morphine in a matter of seconds.

By the time she'd done another set of obs and drawn the blood Alessandro had requested, Ellie was already feeling relief. 'Better?' Nat asked.

'Oh, God, so much better. Thank you.'

The curtain flicked back and Alessandro poked his head in. 'Surgeon will be here in twenty minutes.'

Both the women nodded and Alessandro disappeared again, flicking the curtain back in place.

Ellie looked at Nat. 'That man is totally dreamy.

He can park his Italian leather shoes under my bed any day.'

Nat laughed, understanding the sentiment totally. She felt a surge of female pride, like that of a lioness, that Alessandro's shoes were firmly parked under her bed. Or hers under his, anyway.

'Seriously, seriously gorgeous,' Ellie babbled. 'You could just eat him with a spoon, couldn't you? He doesn't have a ring—is he married?'

Nat suppressed the sudden urge to turn on her patient and growl *Back off, sister* as a sudden shard of jealousy sliced through her. Her patient was smiling like a goon and her voice was a little slurred. Nat reminded herself it was the morphine talking.

'Drugs have obviously kicked in, then,' Nat said, forcing lightness into her voice. 'I'll be back with the surgeon. Here's your bell if you need me for anything.'

Nat stepped out of the curtain and took a few deep breaths. Alessandro looked up from the desk at the same time her gaze fell on him and he blasted her with a dose of heavy-lidded heat. Every cell in her body leapt to attention.

'Nat, I've just put a Mrs Rothbury into cube ten,' Imogen said as she bustled by.

Nat dragged her eyes off Alessandro but not before she noticed a small smile touch his beautiful lips. 'Right. Cube ten. Check.' And she turned away without daring to look at him again.

It was like that for the rest of the shift. Wherever she was—he was.

Smiling at her with those private eyes as she handed over the twenty-six-year-old male who had accidentally ingested sterilising tablets instead of aspirin.

Brushing his fingers against hers as she handed him the chart of the forty-nine-year-old-woman who was having an allergic reaction to an unidentified substance.

Watching her intently as he moved his stethoscope around the chest of a twenty-year-old-male complaining of shortness of breath.

Grabbing her hips and lingering a little too long as he passed behind her in the cramped confines of a lift as they transported a thirty-six-year-old female who had suddenly gone blind in her right eye to CT scan.

And calling her Nathalie every chance he got.

By the time she was halfway through her shift, Nat's body was humming with desire like a damn tuning fork. He was everywhere and each hour cranked the anticipation up another notch. She doubted they'd get any sleep at all tonight.

Just after lunch Nat opened the curtains to cube nine and greeted her next patient. Seventy-two-year-old Mr Gregory, a five-year prostate cancer survivor, was complaining of hip pain. 'Hello, Mr Gregory, my name's Nat. Pleased to meet you.'

Her patient gave a loud hoot. 'Ron, please. Mr Gregory reminds me of my teaching days and as much as I loved it I'm damned pleased I'm not doing it any more.'

Nat laughed. He was a sprightly guy, tall and snowy-haired with crinkles around his eyes like he enjoyed a good laugh and clear blue eyes that contained a wicked sparkle.

'Ron it is.'

'Sorry to be such a damn nuisance. Bloody GP's making a fuss about nothing.'

Nat could hear a strained note in his voice and sensed that beneath all the sparkle and bravado Ron was a worried man. 'Better to be safe than sorry.'

'Hmph!'

Just then Alessandro pushed back the curtain and entered, and Nat felt the wild clenching of her stomach as his presence filled the cubicle. His gaze on her was brief but no less cataclysmic before turning his attention to his patient. 'Mr Gregory, what seems to be the problem today?'

Nat tried to listen to the examination but it was kind of hard to hear over the roar of her hormones. Even the way he doctored was sexy. He listened, he didn't assume or begin with preconceived opinions. He put his patients at ease. He let them talk and gently herded them back with a pertinent question if they wandered off track.

Alessandro put the stethoscope in his ears and Nat helped Ron get into a sitting position so Alessandro could listen to both back and front.

'I see you're not married, missy,' Ron said as he dutifully breathed in and out. 'Are young men blind these days or just plain stupid?'

Nat laughed. She was conscious that Alessandro needed Ron to be quiet and also that he could hear every word magnified through the bell of the stethoscope. 'Good question.'

'Or maybe you're just holding out for a more mature gent? Very wise. Take my generation, we know how to treat a lady.'

Nat laughed again. She was used to patients flirting with her, particularly men of Ron's age. She knew the drill. It was a bit of harmless banter to pass the time and take their minds off their problems. And if it helped distract Ron for a while then it would have served its purpose.

'What do you reckon, missy?'

'Well, now, that depends. What subject did you teach?'

'English.'

'Ah.' Nat sighed. 'I had the hugest crush on my high-school English teacher.'

'I see you're a woman of very good taste.'

Alessandro frowned as he finished listening to Ron's chest and eased the man back down. His patient was openly flirting with Nat and it was frankly annoying.

'He used to quote poetry all the time. I think I was a little in love with him.'

'Poetry? I can quote you poetry. Who's your favourite? Shakespeare? Shelley? Browning? Wordsworth?'

Nat tapped the man's wedding ring. 'Oh, and what would your darling wife say to that?' she teased.

'Ah, well as long as it was Shelley she'd probably forgive me. She's a sucker for Shelley.'

Alessandro blinked as Nat laughed and patted her patient's hand. A surge of undiluted jealousy spiked his bloodstream and he suppressed the urge to pick up Nat's hand and move it away from Ron's vicinity.

'We'll get an X-ray.'

Nat looked up, startled at the steely note in Alessandro's voice. Gone was the incendiary stare and the soft smile on his full lips. His mouth was a bleak slash and the planes of his face looked harsh and forbidding once again.

'I'll organise it.' He nodded at Ron. 'Excuse me.'

Nat frowned as they watched Alessandro leave. 'He's a bit of a grumpy old so-and-so, isn't he?' Ron dropped his voice an octave or two and gave her a sly wink.

Nat gave him a weak smile. 'I think he's just a little distracted.'

She did a set of obs on Ron, chatting with him a bit more about his heyday as an English department head. Then Nat excused herself, assuring Ron she'd be back shortly. Ellie was going to Theatre to have her appendix removed in half an hour and she needed to get her prepped and her pre-med given.

She headed to the small linen cupboard that was situated halfway down the main corridor that ran behind the cubicles for a theatre gown and hat. Alessandro strode towards her from the opposite direction. His powerful thighs made short work of the distance as he stalked closer.

His eyes commanded hers and held fast. She felt like he'd hypnotised her and she was powerless to resist as they moved inexorably closer. Even though his face was grim and his beautiful mouth, capable of such eroticism, looked almost savage.

They drew level and she frowned at him. 'Are you okay?'

Okay? He felt unaccountably not okay. A cold fist was lodged under his diaphragm as a primal emotion he couldn't put his finger on dripped icy poison into his bloodstream. He felt edgy and… tense. Like he needed to prowl. Or maybe go and hunt something…

Alessandro looked around the corridor. Satisfied no one was watching, he grabbed her arm and pulled her into the nearby linen closet, shutting the door.

Nat pulled her arm out of his grasp, jostling her even closer in the tiny room usually only meant for one person. She glared at him as the stuffy air, heavy with the smell of starch, tickled her nostrils.

'You like to flirt with other men?' he rasped.

Nat blinked. His accent sounded more pronounced and, glowering down at her, his gaze as glacial as black ice, he'd never looked more Italian.

'He's seventy-two, Alessandro,' she grouched, not quite believing she was having this conversation. 'He's worried, scared the cancer has come back. He needs someone to look at him as a person, not a chart number or a medical condition. It's harmless.'

Alessandro understood what she was saying. Hell, he even empathised. With any other nurse he would have applauded it. But not her. When she did it he felt the caveman deep inside roar to life. She was his. And he didn't care how crazy it was.

Without hesitation he backed her against the shelves, hands imprisoning her shoulders, and swooped his head down. Their lips met with a sizzle and his mouth opened wide, his tongue thrusting inside her already welcoming mouth. When she responded with a moan he pressed his body against hers harder so she was in no doubt that he desired her and she was his.

He pulled away as abruptly as he had pounced, taking a step back which was as far as the confines of the room would allow. His ragged breathing mingled with hers and filled the space as each stared at the other and caught their breath.

'Don't flirt with anyone, *bella*. I don't like it.' And then he turned, opened the door and left.

Nat reached for the shelf behind her as her knees wobbled and she practically swooned. She should be furious at such liberties. At such Neanderthal behaviour. But she didn't think she'd ever been on the other end of such a blazing kiss and frankly she was too turned on to do anything other than stare at the empty space and grin stupidly.

Nat was slightly preoccupied when she picked Julian up from the crèche that afternoon. Alessandro's kiss still blazed a tattoo on her lips and all she could think about was the coming night.

'I think he's coming down with something,' Trudy commented. 'He's been so much more interactive lately but today he was really quiet. He didn't eat much at lunch and he feels a little warm. We have had a couple of kids here coming down with flu.'

All thoughts of the night fled as concern rose to the fore. Nat placed her hand on Julian's forehead. He did feel a little on the warm side. She knelt beside him. 'Are you not feeling very well, matey?'

Juliano shook his head. 'I feel sore all over.'

His usually bright little eyes looked dull and his cheeks were flushed. 'Are your ears sore?'

Juliano shook his head. 'No.

'Your throat? Does it hurt to swallow? When you eat?'

He shook his head. 'No.'

It did sound like he was coming down with flu. She just hoped it wasn't the dreaded swamp flu that was all over the news. Not that they'd had any cases in Australia to date.

'Come on. We'll get you home and give you something for the fever. Papa can look at you when he gets home, okay?'

Julian brightened a little and Nat's heart did a little flip. It was gratifying to see that, even unwell, Julian was looking forward to seeing his father. They *were* making progress.

They arrived home half an hour later after stopping at the chemist to buy some medication for Julian's fever. Nat administered a dose and ensconced him in front of the television with Flo and strict instructions to stay settled.

Half an hour later Julian was in the kitchen, Flo in tow, seemingly back to his old self.

'I'm hungry.'

Nat quirked an eyebrow. 'You better now?'

Juliano grinned. 'Yep.'

Nat smiled. She hoped so but she wasn't convinced—it could just be the medication talking. Alessandro came home two hours later and she got him to check his son out. He looked in Julian's ears and down his throat and listened to his chest anyway.

'It all seems okay.'

Nat nodded. Alessandro's gaze bathed her in flame and it was hard to concentrate on anything other than him and what she was going to do to him when they were alone later.

By the time Julian was ready for bed a couple of hours later he was feeling warm again and looking a little subdued. She administered some more medicine which he took before Alessandro swept him up in his arms and carried him to bed.

Her heart gave a painful squeeze as Alessandro strode up the stairs with him. The way Julian's skinny little arms clung to his father's neck made her heart sing. They seemed like any other father and son and it was equal parts satisfying and, strangely, sexy.

Nat had a quick shower in her en suite, her thoughts bouncing from Julian's state of health to the thawing of relations between father and son to the smoulder in Alessandro's gaze that caused her skin to tingle everywhere as she scrubbed it.

She dressed in her pyjamas—a pointless exercise—and wandered out into her room at the same time Flo wandered out. Some kind of sixth sense alerted Nat to where her pet was heading. The cat didn't like to intrude on father/son time and seemed to have developed a fascination with Alessandro's bed—not that she could blame Flo.

'Flo,' she growled.

Flo ignored her, disappearing from sight. Maybe it was her mistress's scent, so ingrained in the sheets, that attracted her so strongly. Or maybe it was just some primal recognition of pure animal lust. Whatever the reason, Alessandro hadn't warmed as much to Flo as he had Julian.

She couldn't hear any of the usual giggles or excited interaction coming from Julian's room as she followed Flo's twitching tail down the hallway. Julian was obviously not his usual self.

'Flo,' she whispered at the cat as she crept into Alessandro's room to find her pet casually licking its leg in its favourite spot—the middle of Alessandro's huge bed.

At least the room was looking more lived-in

now than the first night Flo had strutted her way in. They'd all gone through boxes marked *Master* last weekend and personalised Alessandro's room. Julian had been so excited when they'd come across a piece of pasta art he'd done for his father the previous year. When Alessandro had hung it in pride of place on the wall opposite his bed, his little chest had puffed out like a rooster's.

'Flo,' she said again, hands on hips, her low voice holding a note of warning as the cat continued to ignore her. 'You know you're not allowed in here, madam. Alessandro will not be impressed.'

A fine lifting of the hairs on the back of her neck alerted her to his presence a second or two before his arms encircled her waist and she was pulled back into the hard muscles of his front.

'Alessandro doesn't care as long as you're in here too,' he growled in her ear, applying pressure through his arms so she turned to face him.

Nat's breath caught in her throat as his gaze ate her up. There was wildness there, a level of desperation she'd not seen before, not even the first time.

'I've been thinking of you all day, thinking of doing this.'

He didn't give her time to process that. Time to

even suck in a breath as his mouth opened over hers and devoured every atom of oxygen in her lungs. He walked her backwards as she clung to him, dizzy from desire and hypoxia. And then his hands were plucking at the hem of her nightdress until somehow she was relieved of it and then his shirt was pulled out of his trousers and half his buttons were undone.

As they collapsed against the bed her hand had made short work of his zip and she could feel the heavy weight of his erection in her hand. His stubble scratched the soft flesh of her neck as he made his way down and she was parting her legs wider to cradle his hips, urging him closer.

'Alessandro!' She wasn't sure if she wanted him to slow down or go faster. Her mind was a blank. An empty space devoid of any thought, filled only with his scent and the sound of his out-of-control breath.

His mouth closed over a nipple and she cried out, almost convulsing with desire. His hands pushed at her knickers as hers plucked at his trousers. As soon as he had access he entered her and she dug her nails into his back, gasping as he slid home, stretching her, filling her, making her feel more female, more powerful, more helpless than she'd ever felt before.

He pounded into her with frenzied strokes, like a man possessed, and all she could do was cling to his shoulders as each jab built her to a crescendo of lust that contracted her muscles and energised every cell, innervating them to an excruciating awareness.

Alessandro felt the first jolt of his orgasm and crushed her close, burying his face in her neck. The sensation seemed to come from his very soul and he groaned and cried out her name.

Nat wasn't sure when it finished. It seemed to go for ever, suspending them on some plane that floated high even as it faded. It was almost as if she'd lost consciousness and wasn't aware of anything other than him until he grew heavy against her and her body moved involuntarily, protesting the weight.

He rolled off and somehow in the post-coital haze he managed to pull down the bed sheets and relieve them of their barely intact clothes. And then he was surrounding her again, spooning her, pulling her into him, pressing kisses into her neck, touching her breasts and between her legs. It was slower, lazier but Nat felt the heat building again quickly and gave herself up to the moment.

* * *

Several hours later, not long after they'd fallen into an exhausted sleep, Nat woke to a strange noise. Her eyelids flicked open and despite the pull of slumber she was suddenly instantly alert. Her heartbeat boomed in her ears as she strained into the apparent silence.

Then she heard it again. A cry.

Julian!

Careful not to disturb Alessandro, she eased off the bed and groped around for her nightdress. Finding it discarded near the door, she threw it on and headed to Julian's room.

The muted glow from the illuminated fish tank by the window silhouetted Julian's tiny frame as he sat up in bed. 'What is it, matey?' she crooned.

'I've been sick,' he sobbed.

Nat, her brain still cloaked in slumber and her bones still heavy from sexual malaise, reached for the nightlight and snapped it on. Julian's hair was mussy from sleep, his face flushed. She could smell the acidic aroma of vomit and noticed the soiled bed linen.

She sat on the bed beside him and put her arms around his shoulders, noting immediately how warm he felt. 'It's okay, matey. Let's get you cleaned up and give you some more medicine.'

She helped him out of his soiled shirt and groped in his drawer for another. She picked him up and carried him into her en suite where she'd left his medicine just in case it was needed in the night. She administered the medication and then wet a washer and wiped his flushed face.

His fever now seemed to be accompanied by a runny nose and a slight cough. He denied a sore throat and ears and she resigned herself to shelving plans for a day at the beach and spending the weekend nursing him through flu. She carried him back towards his room but he clung to her neck and she didn't feel comfortable leaving him all alone in his bed when he was obviously miserable.

It didn't seem proper to take him into hers. She glanced at the open doorway at the end of the hallway. A memory from her childhood assailed her. She'd been seven and ill from something she couldn't remember now. But she could remember her mother bringing her into her parents' bed and how she had snuggled into her father. He had patted her back and curled his big arm around her and she had felt so safe and secure and loved.

She'd felt like he'd held the cure for cancer in his palm.

It had been just before he'd left them and Nat cherished that memory like it was gold. Sure, her mum had always showered her with TLC when she was sick but without her dad and his big old arm there, she'd always felt a little less loved.

Nat didn't give it another thought. Everyone wanted to feel they were loved when they were sick. It was just…human. She crept into the room and onto the bed and laid Juliano next to his father.

Alessandro stirred and reached for her before he realised the situation. He half sat up and frowned. 'What's wrong?' he whispered.

'Julian's been sick. I think it's flu.'

Alessandro's first instinct was to refuse. Camilla hadn't believed in Juliano sleeping in their bed and her iron-clad opinions were ingrained.

Nat could see the indecision on his face. 'He's four years old. He needs you, Alessandro,' she said gently. 'There's no better place than Papa's bed when you're sick.'

Alessandro looked down at his son. Julian was looking up at him with dull eyes, a kind of hopeless despair giving them an added misery. He smiled down at him. *'Naturalmente il mio piccolo bambino, viene al Daddy.'*

Nat smiled. Her Italian may have been rusty but she knew enough to know Alessandro had consented, and by the look on Julian's face, he knew it too. Alessandro lay down on his side, wrapped an arm around Julian, pulling his little body close. He rested his chin on his son's head.

Alessandro's eyes drifted shut as did Julian's, but not before he'd tucked his hand in his father's. Nat sat and watched them for a few moments, her heart filling with an emotion she didn't want to investigate too closely.

They looked like father and son, like a family. Alessandro, the big protective patriarch, dwarfing Julian whose hand clung tight to his father's. Julian looked how she must have looked all those years ago safe in her father's embrace.

Content, secure, loved.

She sighed and eased herself off the bed, taking one long, last, lingering look before creeping out of the room.

Even as she yearned to join them.

CHAPTER EIGHT

IT WAS amazing the difference a few weeks could make, Nat thought as she sat at a distance and watched Alessandro and Julian build a sand castle together down close to the shoreline. They'd spent the day at Noosa, swimming and playing beach cricket and eating fish and chips at one of the trendy little cafés that lined the boardwalk.

There'd been a subtle shift ever since Julian had been laid up with flu for those two days. Whether Julian had been too sick to find the energy required to stay aloof or whether it'd had been Alessandro's complete attentiveness, they'd come out of it much closer. It was like a bond had been forged—newer and stronger.

And they'd blossomed under it, opening to each other a little more each day. Chatter and laughter filled the house now instead of stilted conversation and the loud buzz of longing.

Julian smiled at his father. Sat next to him on the lounge. Sought him out to tell him things. He looked for hugs and went eagerly into his father's embrace. He'd lost that taut little set to his shoulders. The wary, defeated look that had haunted his features.

And Alessandro stopped looking a hundred years old.

It was heartening to witness and Nat just knew, as the sun beat down on her shoulders, that they were going to be okay. Sure, there would be moments when their grief and sadness would come upon them again, blindside them, but at least now they looked like they'd turn to each other for comfort and support.

At least they'd stopped looking to her for guidance.

'Nat! Nat!' Julian yelled, popping his head up from his all-fours position, waving an arm at her. 'Come and look at what Papa and I built!'

Nat smiled and rose. She'd deliberately taken a back seat over the weeks, pushing the two of them together at every opportunity. It did her heart glad to see father and son doing things together. To see Julian acting like a normal four-year-old. To see Alessandro looking less and less haggard.

But as she walked towards them, their dark, downcast heads together again, beavering away a bit more on their creation, she couldn't deny the tug at her heartstrings and the deep-seated yearning that rose in her chest. She knew it was good, as it should be, but she suddenly felt on the outside. Lonely.

'Isn't it great, Nat?' Julian enthused as she drew level with them.

Nat felt tears prick her eyes and was glad of her sunglasses. It was great on many, many levels. 'It's totally awesome,' she agreed, ruffling his hair.

Alessandro smiled up at her and winked. He was in a sun-shirt that clung to his torso like a glove and boardies that hugged his butt and thighs like a second skin.

'Have I said that's a great bikini yet?' he asked.

Nat gave a half-laugh despite her heavy heart. 'Once or twice.'

His lusty eyes laughed at her and stole her breath. They looked like the smoothed, flattened black pebbles on the beach, warmed by the sun and utterly inviting. She wanted to push him back against the sand and have her way with him. He was easily the best-looking man on the beach.

'Papa and I are going to collect some shells. Can you make sure no one knocks the castle down?'

Nat dragged her shaded gaze away from temptation. She took a breath. Excluded again.

But it was good—so good they were doing stuff together. That Julian wanted to do spend time with his father now, looked to his father first. A few weeks ago he would have wanted her. So this was good.

She swallowed. 'Absolutely, I shall guard it with my life.'

'Come on, Papa,' Julian said as he picked up the bright blue bucket and marched towards the lapping ocean.

Alessandro vaulted upwards his gaze tracking his son's meandering path. 'You'd better wear that bikini to bed tonight,' he murmured, before moving off to follow Julian.

The next day they were all making popcorn in preparation for a movie afternoon. Alessandro and Julian had walked down to the video shop in the morning and chosen a couple of Disney classics.

'Ah, I think that's enough butter, don't you?' Nat laughed as Julian drenched the popcorn.

'Spoilsport,' Alessandro teased, and then gave his son a wink. 'Come on, matey, let's go watch the movie.'

They brushed past Nat, who was momentarily paralysed by the teasing note in Alessandro's voice and the way his sex appeal boosted into the stratosphere when the smile went all the way to his eyes. The fact that he seemed to have adopted the endearment 'matey' for his son was also rather...touching.

The doorbell rang, momentarily distracting her from her ponderings, and she absently called out, 'I'll get it.'

Quite who would be calling on a Sunday afternoon she wasn't sure. Maybe it was the little boy next door? He and Julian were the same age and she had told his mother that he was welcome any day for a play.

The entrance hall was warm and welcoming now with a large colourful rug breaking up the glare of the all-white tiles. Two large paintings decorated the walls on opposite sides and a hall mirror that had come from the ceramic ovens of the Amalfi coast hung by the door.

Last night Julian had helped his father hang a wind chime they'd bought in Noosa. He had passed tools to his father like a scrub nurse would to a surgeon and afterwards they'd stood, necks craned, Alessandro's hand on Julian's shoulder, admiring their handiwork.

The beautiful baby-pink mother-of-pearl discs, brittle and fragile, had cost a small fortune. But Julian had loved how they cascaded like a chandelier. And they certainly gave the entranceway a touch of mystique.

Nat opened the door. The person standing there was far removed from a little boy and very definitely Italian. He was tall and bronzed like Alessandro with an easy grin that emphasised killer dimples and a wicked glint to his brown eyes that would have put a pirate to shame.

So this is what Alessandro would have looked like had grief not hardened his features and permanently furrowed his forehead. The grin on the stranger's face quickly faded and Nat realised that not only was he staring at her rather fixedly but he was also frowning.

'Can I help you?'

As if he knew he'd been caught staring he recovered quite well and shot her a dazzling smile. 'Er…hi? I think I might have the wrong house. I'm looking for Alessandro Lombardi.'

The accent was like Alessandro's too and there was a similarity to this man that told Nat he was some sort of relation. She tried to ascertain his age. His face was smooth, unlined save for a few tiny crows' feet around his eyes, no doubt from laughter and, unlike Alessandro's, his hair was totally devoid of grey. A younger brother, maybe? Did Alessandro have brothers?

Bad time to realise she knew nothing about him. For crying out loud, she still didn't even know his wife's name.

Nat smiled back and held out her hand. 'No, you've got the right place. I'm Nat.'

The man shook it, smile firmly in place, his gaze studying her face intently. It wasn't creepy but it was disconcerting. Maybe he was surprised to find Alessandro shacked up with a woman so soon after his wife's death?

She opened her mouth to explain, feeling unaccountably depressed as their hands disconnected. But what exactly could she say? She turned her head and called out, 'Alessandro!' He could explain. Maybe he knew what the hell they were doing.

Alessandro appeared in a few seconds, his face lighting up like she'd never seen before. 'Valentino! *Il mio cugino! Così buon vederlo!*'

Nat understood enough to know the stranger's name was Valentino and they were cousins. She watched as the men embraced and Alessandro kissed both of his cousin's cheeks. It was surprisingly sexy. She'd always loved that about Italian men. The way they so openly expressed their affection, no matter which gender.

That just didn't happen in Australian society. And she couldn't help but feel it was the poorer for it.

They laughed and clapped each other on the back and then embraced again. Nat was jealous of their easy affection and she looked away as if she was intruding on an intimate moment.

'Valentino, I'd like you to meet Nathalie.' Alessandro looked down at her. He could see the confusion in her gaze and he smiled at her. 'Nathalie, this is my cousin, Valentino Lombardi. All the way from London via Roma.'

He clapped Val on the back again. Considering they'd practically grown up together, it was wonderful to see him. Val had emailed last week to say he would be in town some time in the next month for an interview but he hadn't expected him so soon.

'Nathalie.' Valentino reached for her hand and kissed it. 'It's a pleasure to meet you.'

Nat blinked at the old-fashioned greeting. She got the feeling that Valentino Lombardi was an incurable flirt. Had she not been totally immersed in Alessandro, she might have even been charmed. But Valentino seemed like a boy in comparison.

More like Julian than Alessandro. Too...carefree. Too...casual for her tastes.

'Come in, come in.' Alessandro ushered his cousin inside. 'Julian will be dying to see you.'

As if he'd been called, Julian suddenly appeared. 'Uncle Val?' He looked at the person in the doorway for a second, not quite believing who it was. 'Uncle Val!'

'Juliano!' Valentino held out his arms and the little boy ran straight into them. *Il mio ragazzo caro, meraviglioso vederlo!*

Julian hugged his uncle's neck tight. 'I missed you, Uncle Val.'

'And I you, *bello bambino.*'

'I'm not a bambino,' Julian denied hotly.

Valentino roared. 'Of course not. *Scicocco me!*'

Nat watched the family reunion, feeling even more on the outside than ever. 'I'll just go and put on a pot of coffee,' she murmured, pointing in the direction of the kitchen and taking her leave.

Alessandro and Valentino watched her go. Valentino turned shrewd eyes on his cousin. 'Alessandro, *che cosa state facendo*?'

Alessandro looked at Val's furrowed brow.

Good question. What the hell was he doing? *'It' indennitia di s.'*

Val rocked Julian in his arms. 'Fine?' He raised his eyebrows. 'She's the spitting image of—'

'Conosco che l'fare di m,' Alessandro interrupted. He did. He did know what he was doing.

'Fate?'

Was he sure? Yes, he was. 'She's nothing like…' Alessandro couldn't say her name. Not in front of his son. *'You il ll vede,'* he explained.

And Val would see. Alessandro knew it would only take his cousin a few minutes in Nat's company to see she was nothing like Camilla. Not remotely. He didn't see the physical resemblance any more. He couldn't even remember the last time it had struck him.

They moved into the lounge and Val stayed for the afternoon, drinking coffee and beer and reminiscing. Alessandro felt a familiar spike of jealousy as Julian sat so eagerly, so naturally on Val's lap. He'd always adored his Uncle Val.

It had taken for ever to build up the same rapport with his son. But, then, he supposed Julian had always associated wild and carefree Uncle Val with fun and good times. And Julian, beneath everything that had happened, beneath the sadness and grief, was still a four-year-old boy.

And Uncle Val's lap was only temporary. Before too long his son switched places and had crawled onto his lap, content to listen to Val from the shelter of his father's arms. Alessandro looked over at Nathalie, his gaze triumphant, and she smiled back at him with understanding eyes.

He doubted they ever would have got where they were without her.

Nat left them to it as much as possible. It was another of those family-type events that were important to Julian. Important to them both to bond as a family, and she didn't want to intrude. Of course she caught snatches of conversation as she came and went, both in English and Italian, and it was obvious the cousins were close.

She remembered now that Alessandro had mentioned Val to Paige all those weeks ago. Was it Val's mother who was the deaf aunt he'd mentioned? The one he'd spent a lot of time with growing up? His second mother?

She guessed that explained their affection.

At one stage she caught the tail end of a conversation about women. Alessandro had obviously asked if there was anyone special in Val's life. Along with a hearty laugh, he got this response. 'The word is full of beautiful women, Alessandro. Why limit yourself to just one?'

It was pleasing to see Alessandro shake his head.

She asked Valentino to join them for tea but he excused himself citing jet-lag and the need to prepare for his interview in the morning. Alessandro and Val made plans to meet for lunch tomorrow.

As they stood to say their goodbyes Alessandro's pager beeped. He took it off his belt. 'Looks like we've just had our first confirmed case of swamp flu.'

Nat winged an eyebrow. 'Where?'

'Victoria.' He embraced Val again, doing the very European double-cheek peck. 'Do you mind if Nathalie sees you to the door? I really need to ring work.'

'It will be my pleasure.' Val grinned.

Alessandro glanced at him sharply as Nat headed for the door. Valentino, much like his name, was an incorrigible flirt. But this woman was off limits. Val was charming and despite there being only six months between them, used his younger years and baby face to his advantage. '*Recidi*, Valentino,' he growled low but steady.

Val looked at Alessandro's flinty obsidian eyes and nodded his head slightly. '*Naturalmente.*' And he followed Nat out of the room.

Valentino joined her by the door momentarily

and she smiled at him, holding out her hand. 'It was nice meeting you,' she said.

Val took her hand and once again turned it over and kissed it. 'Thank you, *bella*.' He released her hand and looked at her for a long moment. 'Alessandro and Juliano are doing well. Much better than the last time I saw them. You're good for him, I think.'

Nat blushed at the speculation in his gaze. 'Oh, no, it's not like that. I'm just…helping out until my place is built.'

Val gave her a small smile and bowed. *'Arrivederci.'*

And then he was gone but she was left in no doubt that Valentino Lombardi hadn't believed her for one single moment.

Nat and Julian were sitting on the lounge, watching the television, when Alessandro rejoined them. 'Is it bad?' she asked.

'No.' Alessandro shook his head and sat beside them. Julian automatically crawled into his lap and he unconsciously opened his arms to accommodate his son. 'Fit, healthy forty-year-old male. But there'll be more.'

Nat watched the easy affection between them

and her heart swelled. 'Had he been travelling?'

'Yes. He's just got back from South America. They're chasing down his fellow passengers and his other contacts now.'

Thanks to geography swamp flu, a mutant form of influenza A, had, until today, been kept from Australia's shores. But it had been declared a pandemic by the World Health Organization and there were protocols that had to be followed.

Julian's thumb had crept into his mouth and he giggled at something on the television. Alessandro rubbed his chin against his son's hair, his arms momentarily tightening around his little body. 'It was good seeing Uncle Val again, yes?'

Julian's thumb slipped out as he turned and looked at his father. 'Oh, yes. I love Uncle Val. I like being called Juliano.'

Nat watched Alessandro's smile slip a little and prayed he'd tread carefully. The first day they'd met he'd reprimanded her for using the Italian version of his son's name, citing his dead wife's preference for it to be anglicised. She could tell then it hadn't been his choice but he was just trying to stick with the wishes of the woman who had given his son life.

'You like that, *il mio piccolo bambino*?' Julian

nodded enthusiastically. 'You know Mummy liked you to be called Julian.'

Nat held her breath. She'd rarely heard Alessandro talk about Julian's mother with him. Occasionally, as they'd emptied the boxes they'd come across something and Julian had mentioned his mother. Nat had encouraged it, had encouraged Alessandro to facilitate it. After all they should be able to talk about the woman they both loved so dearly. But neither seemed keen to talk openly.

Using the 'm' word now seemed like another good step forward in their relationship. Julian nodded. 'I know. But I like Juliano better.'

Alessandro raised his eyes to Nat. They looked like polished river stones—black and glassy with emotion. She could see the rush and tumble of feelings there as they swirled around. Would he insist on sticking to Camilla's dictates or would he follow his son's lead?

Alessandro looked down at his son, his heart stretching in his chest, growing bigger, like a balloon ready to burst. He'd expected tears, withdrawal, a return to the sadness at the mention of Camilla. Not a matter-of-fact reply.

'I can...' He hesitated and looked at Nat. She

nodded at him and he continued. 'I can call you Juliano too, if you like.'

Both Alessandro and Nat held their breaths this time as they hung on Julian's reply. The boy simply nodded, said 'Okay', stuck his thumb back in his mouth and returned to watching the television.

Alessandro let out his breath. He looked at Nat who was blinking back tears. She smiled at him and he wanted to pull her close, put his arm around her and snuggle her in beside them, feel her head drop onto his shoulder. But Nat's very sensible insistence that they keep their relationship from Julian...*Juliano*...stopped him.

So he smiled back at her instead and mouthed, 'Thank you.'

Alessandro's elation didn't last long. By the time he'd finished reading to Julian—*Juliano!*—he was seething with frustration. It shouldn't be this hard to call his son by the name he had been christened with. It shouldn't feel so unnatural. He wanted to kick things, yell, shake his fist at God.

He wanted Nat. He wanted to tumble her into bed, pound into her, make all the thoughts that circled endlessly in his head, like vultures around prey, go away. She'd help him to forget, if only for a few hours. She always helped him forget.

Nat was coming out of her shower when Alessandro grabbed her, pulling her naked body hard against his, lowering his head to claim her mouth in a kiss bordering on savage. She responded instantly, twisting her head to give him all he needed, clutching at his shirt for purchase as the power of the kiss almost knocked her backwards. She gave way to his questing tongue, opening to him, and he growled triumphantly low in his throat.

He pulled back slightly, his breathing harsh, his hands kneading her bare buttocks. 'I need you. Now.' He was so close his lips brushed hers with every word.

Nat could feel his hardness even through the layers of his clothes and her eyes practically rolled back in her head as she fought the urge to rub herself against him like some half-crazed feline. He was so close and the smell of him, the taste of beer on his breath, his mere presence was intoxicating. She could barely think for the pheromones that were clogging her senses as their chests heaved in and out, loud in the quiet of the house.

But she knew something was wrong. He'd been

so happy earlier, had gone into Juliano's room with a spring in his step. And now he was looking at her with trouble tainting the lust and desire.

She pushed against his chest. 'What's wrong, Alessandro?'

Alessandro's arms tightened around hers momentarily and then he sighed and stepped back. Damn her for being so shrewd. He raked a hand through his hair as his gaze raked her body. Despite his inner turmoil she was butt naked in front of him and he wanted her. 'Nothing,' he dismissed, reaching for her.

Nat stepped to the side, evading his touch. 'Alessandro.'

He heard the warning note in her voice despite the mesmerising sway of her breasts as she moved. Then she shook her head at him, rolled her eyes, reached for her nightdress at the end of her bed and threw it on over her head.

'Better?'

Alessandro shot her a grudging smile. 'No.' She sent him a reproving look and crossed her arms. He sighed and felt for the edge of her bed as he sat down. 'It feels so strange calling him Juliano. And it shouldn't. *Inferno!* He's half Italian, for goodness' sake. It should come naturally.'

He felt suddenly impotent, despite the raging

hard-on in his pants. Pushing off the bed, he stalked around the room. Damn Camilla and their screwed-up relationship.

He turned to face Nat, rubbing at his forehead. 'He was christened Juliano.' He dropped his hand. 'Camilla insisted on it.'

Nat stayed very still. Camilla. So that was her name. She frowned. 'So why Julian?'

Alessandro snorted. Because it was just one of the ways Camilla had screwed with him, made him pay. But he couldn't say that to Nat because as far as she was concerned he was still in love with his wife and what kind of a man did it make him to admit he wasn't? Admit he'd never loved her in the first place?

He sighed. 'It's a long story.'

He looked sad and defeated and she felt dreadful that he'd gone from being so happy to deeply troubled. Had Valentino's arrival dredged up old, painful memories?

'Can we please just go to bed? I want you.'

Nat's stomach clenched at his blatantly sexual request. She'd hoped he'd take this opportunity to get some stuff off his chest but just because he finally uttered her name it didn't mean he was going to open up about Camilla.

A stronger woman would have pushed harder. A

stronger woman would have insisted they have it out for once and for all. But the way he expressed his desire, the way he looked at her with those wounded eyes, she knew she'd give him anything. She pulled the nightdress up over her head and opened her arms to him.

Much later in his bed, Nat lay draped down his side, her head on his shoulder, his fingers absently running up and down her arm. Sleep hovered around them in a post-coital haze that was both energising and paralysing at the same time.

She rubbed her cheek against his shoulder, revelling in its warmth and their combined aroma. Her hand was resting on his belly and she trailed her fingers up his chest. 'Val looked at me very strangely this afternoon when I opened the door.'

'He was probably trying to work out how available you are,' Alessandro murmured. The mere thought punched him in the gut, even though he knew the real reason his cousin had given her such a strange look.

'You seem close.'

Alessandro smiled. 'We grew up in the same village. Our fathers were brothers. My parents, they were very...passionate people...they argued, a lot. They split up and got back together and split up and got back together. They were up and down like yo-yos. I would get shuffled to Aunty Rosa's when things were in upheaval. Which was often. It didn't matter that she was deaf or had six kids of her own, she always took good care of me. She and my uncle had this totally different relationship. Ben adored Aunty Rosa.'

'Did you have siblings?'

'No. Just me. Which was probably a good thing.' Even though as a kid he had yearned for siblings like Val. Someone to share the burden. 'My father finally left for good when I was fourteen and my mother really fell apart. We both moved in with Rosa after that.'

Nat heard the dull ache in his voice and felt it all the way down to her soul. She rolled on her stomach and propped her chin on Alessandro's chest. 'Did you miss your father?'

Alessandro dragged his gazed from the ceiling to mesh with the warm welcoming glow of hers. 'Not really. I barely knew him. He travelled with his work a lot. He wasn't exactly a hands-on father. He left it up to my mother mostly. And then when he was home they were usually arguing.'

Nat's heart broke for him. Her own memories of her father, before he'd walked out, couldn't be any more different. Maybe that explained Alessandro's clumsy fathering. No solid role model. Maybe he too had left it up to Camilla.

'I'm surprised you married at all with that kind of history.'

Alessandro looked away from her knowing eyes, his fingers stilling on her arm. If only she knew. It had never been his intention to marry. He'd been more than happy playing the field and having a damn fine time doing so. His childhood had cured him of the romantic notion of finding 'the one' and he'd been merrily working his way through the rest.

And then Camilla—clever, sexy, cool-as-ice Camilla—had fallen pregnant. Deliberately.

He looked back at the ceiling, his fingers resuming their feather-light strokes. 'You sound like you talk from experience. Are your parents divorced too? Is that why you haven't ever married?'

Nat shut her eyes as he firmly changed the subject. She'd obviously pushed him far enough for one night and he'd revealed all he was going to—which was a hell of a lot more than she'd known to date. They didn't do this—talk. They had sex until they fell into exhausted slumber. Talking had never been high on their list of priorities. But suddenly she wanted to know everything there was to know.

She sighed and turned on her side again, draping her arm across his chest, her leg over his thigh as she pondered his question. She didn't want to talk about herself but maybe if she did, he might open up some more about himself.

'My father left when I was eight.' Her words fell into the silence and she felt Alessandro's finger falter temporarily before starting up again. 'No warning. He'd been having an affair for a year and the other woman, Roxanne, was pregnant. So he just…left.'

Alessandro heard the slight wobble in her voice and tightened his arm around her. 'I'm sorry.'

Nat shut her eyes. Why after all this time was the devastation still so potent sometimes? 'It was never the same after that. I spent time with him and Roxy and the kids over the years, Mum made sure of it. I have two wonderful half-brothers. But it was like he'd moved on from me. Sure, he still loved me, I knew that, but he just stopped being a father to me, like I stopped being his responsibility.'

Nat swallowed the lump that had lodged in her throat. It had been a long time since she'd thought about this stuff. 'He had his new wife and his boys and I was just always…an afterthought. The old love and affection we had was gone. He became withdrawn from me, emotionally distant, and I always felt like—still do, I guess—that I had to prove I was still worthy of his love.'

It didn't take Alessandro long to figure out why Nat had felt such an instant rapport with Juliano. When he looked back now at the distance between him and his son not that long ago he cringed. Thankfully she'd been here to show them the way.

'It must have been hard for you to watch Julian…' Alessandro shook his head. '*Juliano*. In the beginning.'

Nat nodded. 'I could see the way he looked at you with such longing and it reminded me of the way I used to look at my dad after he'd left. I know the situation was different with you two, that grief was involved, but…'

'It's okay,' Alessandro assured her. 'I knew we were in trouble, I just didn't know how to fix it.' He kissed her forehead. 'And then you came along.'

Nat smiled and snuggled closer. 'Super-Nat to the rescue.' Alessandro chuckled and her heart filled with the sound of it. 'Pity I wasn't so good at fixing my own problems.'

'Is this about the man you talked about in the lift that day? You said it had become untenable.'

Nat nodded. 'He was newly divorced when I met him and that was probably my first mistake. But he was so sad, so knocked around by life and so kind and caring and he was so happy to be happy again, with me, I fell in love with him. He was endearing.'

Which was exactly why being here with Alessandro was stupidity. Alessandro and Juliano were just history repeating itself. Except it was worse. Rob and his wife had chosen to separate. Alessandro hadn't chosen for his wife to be taken from him.

'So what happened?'

'His ex-wife was in his life, our lives, a lot.'

'You didn't like her?'

'I liked her fine. But I don't think either of them ever really let go. He spent more and more time with her, making excuses to see her. A leaky tap. A family wedding. A Valentine's Day meltdown. And after years of coming second to her I just couldn't do it any more.'

'That does sound untenable.'

Nat shut her eyes, the skin on her arms turning to goose-bumps as Alessandro drew circular patterns with his fingers. It had been awful. A long slow death, hanging on, hoping things would change.

'C'est la vie.' She shrugged. 'By the end there wasn't really any love left. Just hurt. I'm over it now.' She didn't want to talk about Rob any more. Or her father. It was his turn.

'What about your wife? Camilla? How did she die?'

Alessandro's fingers stopped abruptly. He couldn't talk about Camilla. Not to her. Not to anyone. He could barely utter her name without waves of guilt pinning him down. She had no idea how much it had cost him to say her name earlier.

He shifted, displacing her temporarily, and then moved over her, settling his pelvis against hers. 'I think we've talked enough for one night, don't you?' And he lowered his head, dropping a string of tiny kisses up her neck and across her jaw.

Nat should have protested. God knew, she wanted to know everything about him but she felt her body respond to his weight and his smell and the way his mouth found all her sensitive places. And did she really want to know about the perfect Camilla and their perfect love? Hadn't she had enough of that in her last relationship?

So she didn't push him away and insist on

talking. She didn't get huffy. She didn't get up and leave his bed. Instead, she shut her eyes and let him sweep her away to the place she knew he could take her.

There'd be enough time for talking when she moved out and their relationship came to an end.

CHAPTER NINE

THE following Thursday afternoon Nat led Alessandro into cubicle fifteen to examine a thirty-eight-year-old woman complaining of a sore leg. She had her nine-month-old baby boy with her, who was crying and irritable.

Alessandro smiled at the rather harried-looking woman who apologised about the noise as she jiggled the babe on her hip. 'He's picked up a bit of a cold so he's not exactly a happy camper at the moment.'

'That's okay…' he searched for the patient's name on her chart label '…Nina. What seems to be the problem?'

'I've got this really sore leg,' Nina said.

'Why don't you give the baby to Nat and hop up here so I can have a look?'

Nat smiled at Nina and the baby and held out her arms. 'What's his name?' she asked.

'Benji.'

'Come on, Benji. Let's give Mummy a bit of a break.'

The baby went willingly enough, sneezing three times during the transfer. 'Bless you, bless you, bless you,' Nat cooed, stroking the baby's warm forehead as she settled him on her hip and began swaying.

Alessandro was momentarily distracted as he watched Nat with Benji. The baby had stopped crying and was looking at her curiously as Nat's ponytail swished with the rocking of her hips. Nat chose that moment to look up at him and he gave her a lazy smile.

She looked good in her uniform. She looked good in shorts. She looked good in her nightdress. And she looked absolutely sensational out of it. He should have guessed she'd look good with a baby on her hip.

Nina, oblivious to their undercurrent, climbed up onto the gurney, swung her legs up on the mattress and proceeded to roll up her jeans. 'That's a bit of a climb, isn't it?' she puffed.

Alessandro's wandering attention returned to his patient. 'So, have you injured yourself in any way?' he asked half his brain still engaged with other thoughts. Images of Nat last night straddling him, smiling down at him.

Nina shook her head. 'My calf's been sore ever since I got off the plane yesterday.'

Suddenly Alessandro's brain snapped into laser-like focus. 'Plane?' He frowned. Painful calf. Air travel. DVT? 'Where did you fly from?'

Nina's brows furrowed. 'Perth.'

Alessandro's gaze sought the area that Nina was rubbing. Perth was only a four-hour flight, which made it less likely for a blood clot to have formed in the deep veins of her leg but it wasn't unheard of. And Nina was a little overweight.

'But I guess that was only a day after our flight from London,' Nina continued. 'Boy was that an awful flight. I was stuck in my seat the whole time with Benji needing to be fed constantly because of the cold playing havoc with his ears. He drank practically all through the flight. It's times like those I wished I'd chosen the bottle over the breast all those months ago. At least his father could have helped out.'

Alessandro's antennae started twitching crazily. Firstly, without even laying hands on her, he could see the swollen red area of Nina's calf. That didn't bode well. But secondly, and perhaps the most importantly, as far as the big picture went, was Benji's cough. It may have seemed quite innocent when Nina had walked in—just another childhood cold. But teamed with the word 'London' it was potentially much more.

Swamp flu was prevalent now in the UK as well as the Americas. The cases they'd had in Victoria had all been carried into the country through international air travel, although not yet from the UK. It was certainly causing all kinds of consternation and hot on the heels of several deaths worldwide some schools with infected students in Melbourne had been shut down as a precaution.

There'd been nothing in Queensland yet but due to the worldwide level six pandemic status there were procedures he had to follow. He didn't think for a minute that Benji had swamp flu but he knew he couldn't let them leave without making sure.

But first things first. Alessandro gently examined Nina's calf, the concentrated area of heat obvious beneath his palm. He felt for a pulse at the back of her knee and also felt for her foot pulses. 'Can you draw you toes back towards your knee?' he asked.

Nina complied, wincing as a hot arrow streaked straight to the centre of her sore calf. 'Ouch.'

'Hmm.' Alessandro urged her back against the pillow. 'I'm just going to feel for a pulse in your groin,' he said. He located the full bound easily. 'Any chest pain?' he asked, taking his stethoscope out of his ears and placing the bell on her chest.

'Nope.'

Satisfied her lung fields sounded clear, he helped Nina up into a sitting position. 'I think you may have something called DVT. Have you heard of it?'

Nina screwed up her face. 'That clot thingy? The one they do the talk about on planes?'

Alessandro nodded. 'Yes. You have the classic symptoms and your forced immobility on the long-haul flight definitely put you at a higher risk. We'll get an ultrasound to confirm the diagnosis.'

Nina looked at him, a worry line between her brows. 'I'm not going to die, am I?'

'They are potentially very dangerous but we've caught this in time and we can treat it.'

Nina looked relieved. 'So...what happens now? Do I have to go into hospital? I have three other kids as well as Benji.'

'I'm afraid it will mean a short hospital stay. We need to start you on a special intravenous drug that helps to thin your blood. And once you have therapeutic levels you go onto an oral form of the drug and you'll need to be on it for several months.'

Nina looked at Nat. 'Holy cow.'

'Can your husband get time off work?' Nat asked. 'Or do you have family to look after the kids?'

Nina nodded. 'My husband is still on holidays till next week. Luckily I have plenty of expressed breast milk in the freezer.'

Nat smiled. 'I'll refer you to our welfare worker as well. She can help with any of the logistics.'

Nina shot her a grateful smile. 'Thanks.'

'There's another thing,' Alessandro added.

Nina raised an eyebrow. 'Oh.'

'I'm going to have to test Benji for swamp flu, I'm afraid.'

Nina's eyebrows practically hit her hairline. 'Swamp flu? You think my Benji's got swamp flu?' She held her arms out for her baby and Nat handed him over.

'No. I don't think he has it. I think in all likelihood he has a common cold but I'm afraid there are certain protocols I'm governed by now because of his symptoms and the fact that he's just come from another country where the infection is prevalent.'

Benji, who was squirming and protesting his mother's tight hold, stopped as soon as Nina relaxed. 'Oh.' She kissed her son's head. 'But what if he does have it?'

'We'll start him on some special antiviral medication, which will help lessen the duration and vigour of the symptoms. We'll have to get the infectious disease team involved who'll track all contacts. The rest of your family will need to go into home quarantine immediately—just in case.'

'For how long?'

'Seven days. But we should have the test results back by tomorrow afternoon so hopefully only a day until they come back negative. You'll have to be nursed in isolation too until we know the results.'

'Hell. What a mess.'

'Yes.' Alessandro nodded. That was putting it mildly. 'But, as I say, I really don't think you've got anything to worry about. Okay?' He patted her hand and smiled. 'Let's just take this one step at a time.'

Nina's worried expression dissipated beneath Alessandro's comforting gesture and calm authority. She nodded. 'One step at a time.'

Nat and Alessandro left the cubicle a few minutes later. 'I'll call ID and X-Ray. We'll have to get a mobile ultrasound,' he said. 'Get an urgent

NPA on both of them and move them to an iso cube. Limit numbers in there and make sure anyone going in wears a gown and mask.'

Nat nodded as she prioritised his rapid requests, feeling the thrill of medicine in action. She loved working with him almost as much as she loved sleeping with him.

The next afternoon Nat was smiling to herself as she opened one of the few remaining boxes stacked in Alessandro's formal lounge area. She could hear father and son chattering away as they cooked tea together and she was looking forward to the weekend.

This time with Alessandro and Juliano had been satisfying on levels she hadn't thought possible as she'd watched their journey back to each other. And she was going to miss them when she left.

But, in the meantime, there were still boxes to get through. The progress had been slow as Nat had given priority to activities that kept Juliano and Alessandro together and focused on the future. Going to the beach, heading to the movies, taking a ferry trip on the river, playing soccer in the park.

Sure, going through the boxes was also something they did together and helped them connect.

They talked about the things inside and it was interesting learning about their lives before they'd entered hers. But she was more than aware that it wasn't a task Alessandro relished—the memories, she guessed—so she found it was better in small doses.

Still, as she looked around the house she couldn't deny the sense of accomplishment. Emptying the boxes, decorating Alessandro's house, seeing it turn from an igloo into a warm, welcoming home, also helped by the flowering of the father/son relationship, had been immensely satisfying.

Something that had started out as a way to help, a thank-you to Alessandro for his generosity, had become much more. And seeing the dividends it was paying in every aspect of their lives was very special.

She settled on her haunches next to the nearest box and opened a lid, finding yet another stash of linen. Whoever the mysterious Camilla had been, she'd had impeccable taste. Egyptian cotton sheets and the very best quality hundred per cent duck-down quilts—a bit unnecessary in Brisbane but too beautiful to shove in a cupboard and ignore.

As she reached in to pull out the next sheet her hand knocked against something hard and she peered in. Something was wrapped in the sheet. She felt it—it was about the size of a large book but not as bulky. Was it the elusive photos Alessandro had assured her were in one of the boxes? She'd almost forgotten about them over the intervening weeks and all their distractions.

Nat's heart tripped in her chest as she gingerly unfolded the fabric to find the back of a photo frame staring at her. She felt nervous as her fingers advanced tentatively towards the object. Was she ready to come face to face with Camilla? Her hand shook a little as she turned it over.

She needn't have worried. It was a photo of Juliano as a baby. He was sitting like a little chubby Buddha in a sailor suit with a little sailor hat plonked artfully on his head. He was grinning at the camera, one hand stroking a sleek black cat.

She smiled. She couldn't help it. Juliano looked so happy. Loved, content, secure. Not a worry in the world—as it should be. So different to the boy she'd first met. How unfair was it that in only a few short years after this candid snap his whole world would be turned upside down?

The resemblance to his father also struck her. Looking at Juliano, she had a glimpse at what a young Alessandro must have looked like. Dark hair, dark eyes, olive skin and cherubic lips. She traced Juliano's mouth with her finger, so like his father's. And that sparkle in his eyes. One that she was seeing more and more of in Alessandro's gaze these days.

He must have been a beautiful baby.

She dipped into the box, eager to see more, her hands finding the tell-tale signs of more frames wrapped in sheets. She pulled them out one by one, unwrapping them like Christmas presents, each one a moment captured in time, a window, an insight into Alessandro's life.

Most of the frames held pictures of a solo Juliano at various stages of his life, chronicling his four years. Crawling. Walking. His first birthday party. But there were two with other people. One with an older Italian-looking woman holding Juliano in what appeared to be a christening gown. Alessandro's mother? Or maybe his aunt? Valentino's mother?

And the other with Alessandro on the London Eye, the magnificent Houses of Parliament forming an imposing backdrop. Juliano looked about two and both he and Alessandro were pointing at something outside the glass bubble and beyond the view of the camera. It was obviously a candid shot. Father and son had been caught in fierce concentration, not smiling, their brows wrinkled, their faces frozen in serious contemplation.

It was strikingly similar to how they'd both looked when she'd first met them. Unsmiling, serious. But there was an ease in the older photograph that hadn't been evident then. Their heads were almost touching, Alessandro's hold was loose and comfortable and Juliano's little arm around his father's neck spoke volumes about his innate trust.

Nat dragged her gaze away from the photo and put it aside, delving for more. The next several frames were academic qualifications of Alessandro's. She spent a few moments trying to decipher the formal Italian, practise her rusty command of the language. But it was too academic for her and she put them aside with a mental note to make sure this weekend they tackled Alessandro's office.

The box was almost empty now, with just two folded sheets sitting on top of some plump cushions. Without even having to look further, Nat knew these were the frames she'd been looking for. Finally she'd get to see the woman who had won Alessandro's heart and for whom he still grieved.

Oddly, she hesitated. After weeks of internal speculation about Alessandro's wife she wasn't sure she wanted to know. What if she was simply the most gorgeous creature she'd ever seen? Could her ego stand that? And yet there was a part of her that needed to know and she cursed it. Cursed her innate female curiosity. Her vanity.

What had Camilla Lombardi looked like? Beautiful, no doubt. Glamorous too, she'd bet. She couldn't see Alessandro, a breathtakingly handsome man who must have had his pick of women, marrying anyone less than stunning. Had she been dark and exotic like Alessandro or maybe a glamorous redhead with milky skin and green eyes?

She stared down at the sheets. Was she ready to come face to face with Alessandro's dead wife? The woman who'd claimed his heart. She drew in a ragged breath at how much it hurt to think of him being loved by another woman. How much it hurt to acknowledge that even when he was buried deep inside her, pounding away, his heart belonged to someone else.

Goose-bumps marched across her skin and she rubbed her arms. This was stupid! They were no more than convenient lovers and she had no right to such thoughts. And his wife was dead. Did it matter what she looked like?

She reached for the sheets and pulled them out of the box, unwrapping the first one and refusing to pay any heed to the knot in her gut. She flipped the frame over briskly, businesslike, mentally chastising her hesitancy. Her eyes instantly connected with an eerily familiar pair of blue ones.

And everything in that moment crashed to a halt. Her heart stopped in her chest. Her breath stilled in her lungs. The synapses in her brain ceased to function. The frame fell from suddenly nerveless fingers and slid off her lap. A loud rushing noise echoed in her head and she couldn't hear anything above the roar. It sounded like she was in a wind tunnel or in the centre of a tornado.

A terrible dreadful sense of déjà vu swept through her, paralysing her with its ferociousness.

It wasn't until her lungs were burning, bursting for breath, and her vision started to blacken at the edges that her body kicked into survival mode and took over. Her jaw fell open, her lips, completely independent of her will, pursed into a tight pucker, sucking in a desperate breath.

Nat coughed and spluttered as it rushed in,

abrading her oxygen-starved membranes. She fell forward, extending her arms to stop herself collapsing altogether. She hung her head, eyes squeezed tightly shut as the coarse white carpet pricked at her palms. She gripped it hard as she gasped for breath, for sanity.

She didn't know how long she sat there, fighting for stability in a world that had suddenly tilted on its axis. She panted and rocked on her haunches like a woman in labour waiting for the contractions to stop, for the pain to ease.

It felt like hours could have passed when she finally opened her eyes and the world slowly came back into focus. Camilla's clear blue eyes looked calmly back at her from the frame on the floor. A small smile hovered on the other woman's perfectly made-up lips, like she'd gotten everything she'd ever wanted in life and she knew it.

A splash of moisture fell on the frame and Nat blinked. She felt her cheeks, surprised to find tears running down her face. The same sort of face that looked back at her from the glass. Same blue wide-set eyes, same blonde ponytail, same high cheekbones, generous mouth and pointed chin with the cutesy-pie cleft.

Nat shook her head as her earlier thoughts came back to haunt her. *Did it matter what she looked like?* She couldn't believe it had only been mere minutes ago that she'd been that innocent. That she'd ever been that innocent.

She picked up the frame and stared at the familiar contours of the other woman's face. *They could have been sisters.* Her and Alessandro's dead wife. Their resemblance was uncanny.

The knowledge punched her in the gut.

Nat climbed awkwardly to her feet, clutching the photo, her legs rubbery, numb from sitting too long in her cramped position. She stood motionless staring at the dead woman's face, feeling like her heart had been ripped out of her chest and stomped on. Feeling rage and impotence and desperation in equal measure as the awful, awful truth sank in.

She was in love with Alessandro.

In love with a man who was still so in love with his dead wife he'd chosen a look-alike replacement with no thought to the consequences.

Her sense of loss was so profound not even the sobs that were choking her chest, threatening to strangle her, could find an outlet. She could hear a low kind of keening and knew it was coming from her, but didn't seem to be able to stop.

It was like Rob and her father all over again. Worse. Way worse. She'd had to compete with two women in her life for the affections of men she'd loved deeply. But at least those women had been alive. Tangible. How did she compete with a perfect memory? A ghost?

And, *goddamn it,* why was she always the bridesmaid and never the bride with the men in her life? Why was she always second choice? Wasn't she good enough? Lovable enough? Her father had left her for a new family. Rob had left her for an old one. And Alessandro?

Nat heard a little voice inside her ask the question she'd never allowed herself to ask. Had always felt selfish even thinking it. *What about me?*

'Nat! Nat!'

Nat jerked as Juliano came haring into the room, jumping up and down. She hugged the frame to her chest automatically as Juliano babbled on.

'Daddy and I have cooked the tea. It's his nonna's recipe from Roma and it's so delicious.' He paused, bunched his fingertips together and kissed them for dramatic effect, like Nat had seen Alessandro do the other night in the kitchen. Normally she would have laughed but she was barely taking any of it in.

'He says as long as it's okay by you I can go and play with Flo in the back yard but I have to make sure I wash my hands afterwards before I eat dinner because that just good hygiene.'

Nat blinked, her sluggish brain catching up with Juliano's rapid chatter several seconds later. She noticed some movement in her peripheral vision and glanced up to see Alessandro lounging in the doorway in the half-light like a big lazy cat. She looked at him helplessly. Even now, even knowing what she did, even mad as hell, her body still responded to the blatant sexuality of his.

'Nat!'

Her attention returned to the excited little boy in front of her hopping from one foot to the other. 'That's fine.' She nodded.

'Yippee-ee!' Juliano took off, heading for the lounge room and calling for Flo.

Alessandro pushed off the doorframe and prowled towards her. With Juliano occupied outside he had a hankering to kiss her. Last night seemed forever ago. 'How many boxes to go now?'

Nat's heart boomed in her chest as she read the intent in his black eyes. A part of her wept inside as she realised she'd never kiss him again. She took a step back as he advanced.

Alessandro frowned as he entered the arc of

light spilling across her. She looked pale and shocked, her blue eyes red-rimmed and flashing with pain. 'Nathalie!' He took two quick steps towards her. 'What's wrong?'

Nat took another step back, moving her arm out of the way as he reached for it. He stopped and looked at her, his frown deepening.

Nat released the frame she was holding and turned it around. 'When were you going to tell me about this?'

Alessandro's gaze flicked down to the object he hadn't even noticed she'd been holding in his haste to touch her. Camilla's face stared back at him, her Mona Lisa smile taunting him. So like the woman in front of him. And yet so not.

He shuttered his gaze as the painful memories assaulted him. Their loveless marriage, the argument, the knock on the door. He stuffed his hands into his pockets. 'Ah.'

Nat felt the casual comment right down to her toes. *Ah*? He knew. No what-the-hell-are-you-talking-about? frown. No immediate this-isn't-what-it-looks-like explanation. He knew.

Oh, God—it all made so much sense now. The way Juliano had looked at her that first day like he'd seen a ghost. Followed by Alessandro's own, more subtle but definitely, looking back at it now, stunned reaction later that same day. And more recently, Valentino's double-take.

She shoved the frame at him, pushing it hard into his abdominal muscles and releasing it as his fingers closed around it. 'Is that all you've got?' she demanded. His face was the grim mask of old. She couldn't tell whether he was desperately searching for an explanation to give her or whether he just didn't give a damn.

She scrubbed at her face. 'You know, Alessandro I knew you had an ulterior motive when you asked me to stay. I knew you wanted me to be some kind of substitute mother. But I had no idea what you really wanted was a substitute wife!'

'No!' His denial was swift and certain. Yes, the evidence was damning but how could he explain to her that the physical resemblance was where the similarity between her and Camilla ended? Without going into all the sordid details? Without exposing his guilt and shame? He didn't talk about that. Not with anyone. 'You are nothing like her.'

Nat couldn't tell whether it was an affirmation or an insult. She stabbed her finger at Camilla's frozen face. 'That's not what I see.'

'Trust me,' Alessandro intoned. 'The resemblance is only skin deep.'

Nat snorted. 'Trust you?' She stared at him incredulously. 'Why should I do that? When you haven't trusted me? Hell, Alessandro, you had the perfect opportunity to tell me the night Val visited. I asked you why Val had looked at me so strangely. And you dismissed it.'

Nat shook her head, feeling an edge of hysteria building. 'No wonder you weren't keen for me to find these pictures. Why weren't you just up front with me from the beginning? Why didn't you say, "Gee, Nat, you look freakily like my beloved dead wife"?'

Beloved. She thought he was still in love with his wife. Well, of course, he castigated himself, why wouldn't she? Marriage did imply love and it hadn't even been a year yet.

Alessandro watched as tears splashed down her cheeks. He took a step towards her, the urge to pull her into his arms, to comfort her, overwhelming. But she took another step back from him and it was like a blow to his solar plexus.

He opened his mouth to deny it, her tears clawing at his gut. But how could he say the words aloud? *I didn't love her. I didn't love my wife.* What kind of a man did that make him?

Alessandro shook his head helplessly, wanting to wipe away her despair but shying from the words he knew he'd have to use. 'It's not like that.'

His generic reply cut deep. 'God,' she wailed. 'This is just like Rob all over again. Like my father. Playing second fiddle to another woman.'

She'd bounced back from her father. She'd had the love, understanding and support of her mother and other family. And her sunny personality. And she'd come through the Rob nightmare too—a little more bloodied and battered but still with belief in herself and in others.

But she knew without requiring any deep thought or analysis that her love for Alessandro far outweighed anything she'd ever felt for Rob. The slow gentle realisation of her feelings that she'd experienced with Rob was chicken feed compared to this all-encompassing, bubbling cauldron of desire and emotion Alessandro had hurled her into and been marinating her in for these last magical weeks.

She looked at Alessandro's emotionless face. The only sign that any of this was affecting him was the clench of his jaw. 'Did you ever just want me for me?'

It was a startling thing to admit to herself. But she knew she was right. While she'd been falling in love he'd just been using her body to try and erase the memory of his wife.

Loving the one he was with.

It certainly explained his insatiability. The almost desperate way he reached for her every night. Pounding away deeper, faster, harder, like he was afraid she'd evaporate in his arms if he wasn't constantly touching her.

Alessandro flinched at her accusation. 'I think I've more than adequately shown you how much I desire you.'

She looked at him like he'd just grown a second head. Desire? He might as well have reached into her chest and ripped out her haemorrhaging heart. When you loved someone, desire was just an empty vessel. It meant nothing without love.

'Really, Alessandro? Can you honestly stand here and tell me that every night with me, every insatiable moment, it was about me and not some kind of sick reconnection with Camilla?'

Alessandro felt a rage building inside. He knew she'd been played by men but he'd never use a woman in the way she was accusing. Surely she could see that his desire for her was one hundred percent genuine? 'That I can guarantee,' he ground out. 'When I've been in bed with you there's been no one else. I'd have thought you'd know me well enough by now to know that deep in here.' He tapped her chest.

Nat's heart beat frantically beneath his fingers as if it was trying to touch them. Traitorous organ! She knocked his hand away. 'This isn't about sex, Alessandro. It's about love.'

Alessandro blanched. What the hell did love have to do with it? 'Love?'

Nat flushed. Her chest had swollen with a mix of emotions that threatened to crush her and the truth had tumbled out. She hadn't meant to blurt it like that but she was damned if she was going to back away from it now.

'Yes, Alessandro, love,' she threw at him. 'I'm sorry, I know that this wasn't about love but it happened anyway. I guess I'm not quite as callous as you.'

Alessandro raked his hand through his hair, feeling more and more out of his depth. 'Nathalie…'

Nat shut her eyes and shook her head vigorously. 'No. Don't say anything.' She couldn't bear to hear any platitudes. 'I'll be out of your hair before you know it.'

Alessandro reeled a little more. She was leaving? The thought was shocking. 'But…your place won't be ready for weeks yet. What about Juliano?

You can't just up and leave with no notice. He adores you.'

Nat felt a sob rise in her throat. His son did. But he didn't. Not quite the impassioned plea she'd hoped for, even though somewhere inside she felt a surge of pride that he was at last thinking like a father. Thinking about his child even before himself.

And he was right—leaving Juliano would be heart wrenching too. She loved the boy as much as the father. But at least she knew they now had each other.

She shrugged. 'I'll tell him something has come up and a friend needs me.'

'Where are you going to go?'

Nat didn't have a clue. All she knew was she couldn't stay here another minute. She felt like she was bleeding and it was sure as hell going to make a mess on Alessandro's perfect white carpet.

'I don't know. Paige's maybe. A hotel.' She shook her head. 'Frankly, I don't care. Just away.' She backed up as she spoke. 'Far away from here.'

Alessandro reached out and snagged her arm before she could run away. He couldn't bear the idea of her gone. 'Please don't go. We need you.'

Once it would have been enough. But she was tired of men needing her too much and not loving her enough. Now she knew the true depths of love—its power, its breadth—she knew she couldn't settle for anything less.

Nat shook her head. 'No, you don't. Not any more. You two are going to be just fine.' She pulled out of his grasp, her heart breaking, her soul aching.

The phone rang and they both looked at it, suddenly becoming aware of the surroundings outside their immediate circle of misery.

'You'd better get that,' she murmured, backing away.

Alessandro ignored it. 'Nathalie,' he called after her.

Nat turned away, the desire to run from him crippled by overwhelming misery and the weight of her heart in her chest. The stairs before her suddenly seemed like Mt Everest, her room way beyond at the summit.

Alessandro watched her go. He couldn't remember ever feeling so impotent. But she was asking too much. Love? Didn't she know that he wasn't worthy of her love?

The phone's insistent peeling nagged at him and four angry strides brought him level with the infernal contraption. He snatched it off its cradle.

'Yes?' he snapped.

Nat had almost packed her bag when Alessandro strode into her room. She was crying, tears blinding her progress. Her hands were shaking and her breath occasionally caught on a sob.

'Stop packing.'

Nat gave a harsh laugh. 'Go to hell.'

'That was the ID director from St Auburn's. The baby yesterday we screened for the swamp flu tested positive. As of now we're both on seven days' home quarantine. I'm afraid you're going nowhere.'

CHAPTER TEN

THE only person remotely pleased about their enforced confinement was Juliano. Having never had his father's absolute attention for an extended period, he thought all his Christmases had come at once. He even suffered the daily nasal swabs that were couriered to and from the house with a cheerful disposition.

He was completely ignorant to the suddenly stilted atmosphere between Alessandro and Nat. He didn't notice the strained politeness or the wary avoidance of any kind of physical contact. Not even the absence of laughter or easy conversation penetrated his happy little bubble.

But Nat was excruciatingly aware of it. It was a double loss. Not just the loss of what could have been but what they'd already had. It had been a surprise for her to realise the feelings for Alessandro that had stealthily invaded her every cell were love and a particularly cruel blow to discover it at the very second it was ripped out of reach. It had become crystal clear to her in that moment they'd never be able to return to what they'd had before.

Alessandro had tried to broach the subject again that next morning but she'd cut him off at the pass with a frosty 'Don't'.

She didn't want to hear any platitudes. She didn't want to watch him tie himself into a verbal pretzel with pretty euphemisms. She didn't want to know his justifications. The truth was he had hurt her way more than Rob's or her father's rejections ever had. At least they'd declared their outside interests from the beginning.

Alessandro had been utterly disingenuous.

After three days in home quarantine, or house arrest as Nat had come to think of it, she was at screaming point. If she hadn't been young fit and healthy she might have begun to worry about the constant pain in her chest and the heaviness in her limbs. Her jaw ached from the continuous fake smile she wore and her eyes felt gritty from three nights of crying herself to sleep.

She despised the nightly ritual more than anything. But no amount of internal dialogue castigating Alessandro and his deception derailed the tears. Her mother would say they were healthy, that she was grieving and they were a painful and necessary part of the healing process, but Nat would have done anything to stop them.

She wished she could be more like Paige whose opinion of men since her husband's desertion had always made her wince. Paige wouldn't have fallen for Alessandro. Paige's heart was guarded by barbed wire and thorny bushes a mile thick. Why hadn't she done that to hers? After her father? After Rob? Wrapped it up, protected it? Why had she been lumbered with this damn eternal optimism?

Because even now, despite everything, she wanted him. Every time he looked at her with his black eyes, she felt her pelvic floor muscles shift. Every time he walked by, her nipples pebbled as if he'd brushed his hand across them. Every time he opened his mouth, she wanted to kiss it.

Despite his soul-ravaging betrayal. Despite knowing he didn't feel the same way about her. Despite knowing that every time he looked at her all he saw was his dear, darling Camilla.

She was helpless against his pull. Oh, she hated herself for it but that didn't seem to matter either. Why? Why did love have no pride?

But mostly she was worried. About her willpower. If her belly lurched just at his nearness, how was she ever going to steal herself against him? How was she going to walk out the door? How strong would her resistance be by the end of seven days? Lord knew, it had been three days now since they'd shared a bed and despite how mad she was, she wanted him on top of her and inside her with an almost crazy desperation.

What if he asked her to stay again? Would she sacrifice her integrity and stay? Like she'd stayed with Rob, hoping it would be different? Like she'd held out hope that her father would, one day, remember that he also had a daughter?

No, seven days couldn't come around soon enough. Putting on an act for Juliano was a bigger strain than she'd ever thought it would be. And it felt wrong to lie to him. She knew how it felt to find out you'd been lied to. Only too well.

On the evening of the third day she excused herself after tea. She had a headache and was feeling weary. The sleepless, teary nights were catching up with her.

'You haven't eaten much,' Alessandro commented as he inspected her almost full plate.

She stared at him, absently rubbing her bare arms that had suddenly become covered in goosebumps. 'I'm not very hungry these days.' It was said pleasantly enough for Juliano's ears but her gaze left him in no doubt as to the cause of her poor appetite. She couldn't afford to soften her stand or let her guard down. 'Excuse me.'

Alessandro watched her go, his hands fisting in his lap. He wasn't sure whether he wanted to shake her or kiss her. It had certainly been a long time since he'd tasted her lips and her flushed cheeks and red mouth had drawn his gaze tonight like a moth to flame.

He knew he deserved her contempt. Looking at it from her perspective, his actions must have seemed extraordinarily callous. But he wasn't sure he could stand four more days of the cold shoulder.

It was like his marriage all over again. Constantly pretending everything was all right for Juliano's sake and for those outside their marriage. The stress of projecting the illusion of marital bliss had been a constant drain when it had all been a sham.

'What's wrong with Nat?'

Juliano's question broke into his reverie. He smiled down at his son. 'She's fine.' He smiled. 'Why?'

Juliano shrugged. 'She's really quiet. And she looks sad.'

Alessandro was surprised by his son's insight. They'd both been trying to carry on as normal, to protect Juliano, but he was obviously a lot shrewder than they'd given him credit for. This wouldn't do at all. Surely for four more days they could make more of an effort?

By the time Nat was halfway up the stairs waves of goosebumps were marching across her skin and every footfall jarred through aching hips and knees. She shivered and rubbed her arms, her shoulders protesting the movement. Great! Marvellous. Just what she needed—swamp flu.

Her chagrin with Alessandro vanished as fantasies of a steaming-hot shower took over. If only her room didn't seem so far away. She held onto the rail and gritted her teeth as she hauled herself closer. After a shower she was going to bed. With a little luck she'd sleep for three days and then this whole quarantine thing would be over and she could get as far away from Alessandro Lombardi as was possible.

She entered her room, walking straight past her bed, and started pulling at her clothes, tearing them off, uncaring where they fell. Her teeth chattered as more and more of her body was exposed to the air. She stepped into the shower cubicle and flicked on the taps, shivering as she waited for it to heat up and then gratefully stepping into its fiery embrace.

But still she felt cold, so cold, beneath the spray and she reached for the taps, reducing the amount of cold water till it was practically scalding. She sighed when it finally seemed hot enough, leaning her forehead against the tiles as it seeped into her tissues, her bones, her marrow.

It had been years since she'd had flu and Nat had forgotten how truly horrible it could be. She felt dreadful. Her head ached, her joints felt like they were on fire, her throat was scratchy and she didn't need a thermometer to know she had a high fever.

As if a broken heart hadn't been enough to contend with.

Alessandro left Juliano sitting on the lounge with Flo, watching a DVD, ten minutes later. He needed to talk to Nat, whether she wanted to or not, and he didn't want little ears listening in. He heard the shower as he entered her room and his gaze tracked her path to it from her discarded clothes.

He hesitated for a moment but, hell, he had seen her naked before. They'd showered together numerous times. Had even had hot, wet, soapy sex on more than one occasion. He was damned if he was going to tiptoe around in his own house!

He strode into her en suite, stopping in the doorway to lean his shoulder casually against the jamb. The bathroom was full of steam and even if he'd wanted to catch a glimpse of her wet naked body, the fogged glass made it impossible. 'Maybe I should have installed a sauna in here for you,' he said dryly.

Nat's head shot up and she winced as her neck objected to the sudden movement. 'Get the hell out of here, Alessandro.' She was hoping for assertive but her voice had developed a croak and it sounded more desperate than definite.

'Nothing I haven't seen before,' he drawled.

Satisfied he couldn't see her through the fog, she placed her forehead back against the tiles. 'Nothing you're ever seeing again,' she grouched.

'I want to talk to you.'

Nat shut her eyes as her head thumped. 'Yeah, well, I don't want to talk to you.'

Alessandro's jaw tightened. 'It's about Juliano. It's important. Now, we can do it out here or I can come in there but we *are* having this talk, Nathalie. Now.'

Nat heard the menace in his voice and believed

him. She felt so wretched all she wanted to do was burst into tears but she'd done that too much lately as it was. She was sick of feeling weak and helpless around him. Surely she could stand it as long as they focused on Juliano? And then maybe she could go to bed and sleep for a week.

'Fine,' she muttered, flicking off the taps. 'Pass me a towel, please.' She waited a moment or two and one appeared over the top of the shower stall. She grabbed it and gave herself a brisk once—over, every joint groaning but thankful that the shivering seemed to have been remedied by the hot water.

The fogged screen didn't allow her much of a view but she could see a dark figure looming in the doorway. Nat wished she had the gumption to waltz from the shower completely naked and sail past him with utter indifference. Just to show him what he was missing out on. But she knew she didn't have the guts to pull it off.

'My nightdress is hanging on the rail.'

It too came over and she quickly pulled it on. Her knickers were outside in a drawer—she could worry about them after Alessandro had had his say.

She took a moment to gather herself and then pulled the door open, walking gingerly from the

stall. A blast of cool air hit her heated skin and the
hairs on her arms stood to attention. Her stomach
lurched as she took in his casual stance. His tie
was long gone and his top button was undone.
His sleeves were rolled up to his elbows, baring
strong forearms covered in dark hair. Her already
wobbly knees weakened further. The overhead
light glinted off his hair like moonbeams off a
dark sea.

'If you're going to try and justify what you did,
you're wasting your breath,' she warned as she
pushed past him.

Alessandro counted to ten before he turned to
face her. *No, he wasn't.* It was better this way. Let
her think what she wanted. It couldn't be worse
than names he'd called himself. If this was his
punishment for entering into a loveless marriage,
for the argument with Camilla and its subsequent
domino effect, so be it.

He didn't want neither did he deserve her feelings. He'd squandered love once already and now
he was paying. He didn't expect happiness.

His gaze roved over her face. Her cheeks were
flushed from the hot shower. She looked all pink
and fresh. He could smell soap and he wanted
to pull her close and bury his nose in the place

where her neck met her shoulder. He shoved his hands in his pockets.

'I told you, it's about Juliano,' he said gravely. 'He knows something is up. He's worried about you.'

The thought that Alessandro's precious little boy was worrying about her was touching. She pictured his uptight little face when she'd first met him and knew she couldn't bear to see him so solemn again.

'I was thinking today we should float the idea of me moving out at the end of the week so it's not sprung on him,' she said. 'We'll tell him the unit's finished earlier than expected.'

Alessandro nodded with difficulty. She'd made such a difference in their lives it was hard to believe she'd been in it for such a brief time. Like Mary Poppins. Juliano, who'd already been through a major loss, was going to miss her. So would he. He already missed the smell of her and her warmth plastered to his side as he lay in bed at night.

'Perhaps in the meantime you could act like we haven't been quarantined for ebola?'

Nat glanced at him sharply, each neck vertebrae groaning in protest. 'I beg your pardon?'

'Well, you haven't exactly been your usual

touchy-feely, happy-go-lucky self,' Alessandro pointed out. He missed that the most. The little smiles she'd give him, the brush of her hand on his arm or his back as she went by, the quick automatic ruffle of Juliano's hair.

Nat felt another shiver quake through her abdominal muscles as her ire rose. She wrapped her arms around her middle and glared at him. 'Gee, sorry bout that. I don't know what on earth could have come over me.'

Alessandro watched a spark of anger glitter in her eyes and her cheeks redden further. 'I never meant to hurt you, Nathalie.'

'Yeah, well, you did, Alessandro,' she snapped. 'So you'll have to forgive me if I can't just shake that off and act like nothing happened.'

Her bitterness was tangible and Alessandro felt lower than snake's belly. The last thing he'd wanted to do was hurt another woman. Especially one who had come to mean so much in such a short space of time.

But, damn it, he'd never promised her anything. Certainly not love or any kind of happy ever after. Same with Camilla. She'd known the deal when they'd married. But she'd never tired of turning the screws ever tighter. The weight of his guilt was like a boulder on his chest and sometimes he felt like he could barely breathe.

He was sick of carrying around all that extra weight. He'd let Camilla pile it on him but standing in front of Nathalie he was suddenly utterly over being the guilty party. 'I never asked you to fall in love with me,' he snapped.

Nat's head was throbbing again and her body felt like one giant bruise. It hurt to talk, it hurt to think, but something goaded her on. Maybe it was the flu—she'd never been this bitchy with Rob. After years of sharing she'd just accepted that she couldn't compete with his ex and let him go. But this was like a festering wound and deep inside she knew it needed lancing.

'No, you didn't. It was just about the sex, wasn't it? And what a bonus you got in me, huh?'

Alessandro ignored the edge of hysteria. He'd never seen her so riled. But her assertion that he had just been using her body was way off base. It may not have been love but it had been more than a superficial physical liaison—of that he was certain.

'I think you know I feel more deeply than that,' he said tightly. 'How many times have I shown you these last weeks?'

Nat wasn't sure if it was the fever or his simplistic statement that caused her hysterical laugh. 'Sex?' Her eyebrows practically hit her hairline as her voice rose an octave to almost a squeak. She felt her blood surging through her neck veins and pounding around her head, flushing her cheeks further. Her head felt like it was about to blow off her shoulders.

He had to be joking! 'Sex isn't love, Alessandro. No matter how many times you do it.'

The fervour in her eyes was compelling. '*Inferno*,' Alessandro roared. She was being impossible. 'I only meant—'

'Stop it, stop it, stop it!'

Alessandro and Nat looked down as Juliano hurled himself between them. He had tears streaming down his face and was clutching Flo in his arms.

'Juliano!' Alessandro crouched down and hugged the distressed little boy in his arms. How long had he been watching them?

Nat was speechless. What an awful thing for him to have witnessed. The poor darling had probably never witnessed a man and a woman arguing like this. She felt a rush of light-headedness as she stroked Juliano's head.

Alessandro glanced up at Nat in time to see her sway dangerously. 'Nathalie?'

She heard his voice coming from far away as her vision blackened at the edges, becoming narrower and narrower. 'Alessandro?' she whispered as she stumbled forward.

He reacted quickly, catching her before he was even fully upright. She slumped against him as if her bones had dissolved and he frowned as her heated skin scorched his. *Inferno!* She was burning up. He swept her up into his arms. 'Nathalie?' He shook her gently, her limbs swinging limply rag-doll fashion.

'Papa?'

Alessandro could hear the fear and worry wobble Juliano's voice. Nat stirred and murmured something unintelligible. 'It's okay, matey. She's just fainted.'

Alessandro gave her another shake. 'Nathalie? Are you okay?'

Nat could vaguely hear him. She sighed. It was bliss to have the burden of keeping upright taken from her. 'Damn flu,' she muttered.

'Is she sick, Papa?'

Alessandro looked down at Juliano. 'I think she may have flu.'

Juliano's eyes grew saucer-like. 'Swamp flu?'

'I'd say so.' Alessandro looked at the bits and pieces of paper, the three books and two magazines littering the surface of her bed. 'Come on, Juliano, help me get her into bed.'

Juliano also looked at the bed and then shook his head. 'No. Your bed. When I was sick you let me sleep in your bed. And Nat said there's no better place when you're sick then Papa's bed.'

Alessandro gave him a wry smile. Somehow he didn't think she'd meant it to apply to her. But he looked down into her flushed face. She looked so…still. He couldn't bear the thought of her sick and alone. Plus, given the flu's severity it would help him keep a closer eye on her. She may well hate him for it in a couple of days but Juliano was right.

He grinned down at his son. 'Good thinking, Juliano.' And he strode out of her room with Juliano and Flo trotting behind.

Juliano stayed with Nat while Alessandro went downstairs to get her some of the antiviral medication they'd been given in case one of them did come down with flu. It wasn't going to cure it but hopefully it would reduce the severity and duration. He also grabbed a couple of cold-and-flu tablets he had with his other medicines.

When he returned, Juliano was stroking Flo with one hand and Nat's hair with the other.

'She's still sleeping, Papa,' he said earnestly as Alessandro sat on the side of the bed.

He smiled at his son. 'I imagine she'll be sleepy for a couple of days.' He reached out his hand and shook Nat's shoulder gently. 'Nathalie, wake up. I have some tablets for you.' She didn't move so he shook her a little firmer.

Nat prised her eyes open even as sleep fought to tug them closed. The room was dim and her surroundings were blurry but somehow though she knew she was in Alessandro's bed. His smell surrounded her.

Their smell surrounded her.

She half sat, displacing Flo. 'I shouldn't be in here. I don't want you to catch it.' And for about a million other reasons.

'The best place when you're sick is Papa's bed,' Juliano repeated gravely.

Alessandro smiled. 'Juliano's recent flu will probably be more than sufficient immunity and I got flu in January so don't worry, I reckon we'll be fine. Anyway, it's too late now. If we're going to get it, it's already incubating.'

He opened his palms to offer her the pills and was grateful when she didn't argue any more. He passed her a glass of water to swallow them with. 'The results from your nose swab today should be in tomorrow so we'll know for sure whether it's swamp flu.'

Nat nodded wearily as she sank back into the pillows, her eyes already shut. 'Hmm,' she muttered as she drifted towards a dark abyss.

Alessandro put Juliano to bed a couple of hours later and checked on Nat again. She'd kicked her coverings off and was lying in a fairly good likeness of the recovery position, her back to the door. Her nightdress had ridden up and he could just see a glimpse of bare cheek. He'd forgotten she wasn't wearing any underwear. He strode across the room, pulled the sheet up and got the hell out.

A few hours later he came up again with some more tablets. The sheets were kicked off again but she was much more decent this time, having rolled onto her back, her clothes covering her completely.

He woke her and she roused only enough to swallow the pills and slurp down some water before collapsing back against the sheets again. He pulled the covers up and headed back to his office.

It was well after midnight when he returned to his room for the night. He was tired and couldn't avoid it any longer. The sheets were off again when he entered and he smiled to himself. She was worse than Juliano. He left her as she was for the moment, knowing he'd pull them up when he joined her after his shower.

He lingered under the spray, his mind wandering to the peek of bare flesh he'd had earlier. It seemed like months since he'd touched her intimately. Run his hand over the curve of her bottom, had it snuggled into his groin.

Knowing she was back in his bed and had nothing on beneath her nightdress was having a predictable effect and he quickly turned the hot water off, bracing himself against the cold spray. *Inferno!* She was sick, for God's sake. Feverish and fluey. How dared he let his libido take control?

He towelled himself off briskly and threw on some cotton boxers and a T-shirt then gently eased into bed, careful not to disturb her. She was on her side again, her back facing him. He lifted the sheet over her, his hand touching her arm to gauge her temperature, pleased to find her skin was cool to touch.

Maybe she'd be spared a severe infection and recover quickly? After spending half the night scaring himself senseless by reading swamp flu stats, he hoped so. The thought was comforting anyway and despite doubting he'd be able to sleep at all he actually drifted off with surprising ease.

He woke half an hour later to Nat's shaky voice and groping hands trailing fire down his abdomen.

'I'm s-so c-cold,' she stuttered, her teeth chattering as her body, like a biological homing device, instinctively sought the nearest source of heat.

Alessandro automatically bundled her closer, pulling her into his side, his hand rubbing up and down her arm. Despite her shivering, she felt very hot and he knew she was having rigor.

Nat felt some relief from the cold that bit at her arms and legs and nipped at her fingers and toes as she absorbed the warmth from Alessandro's body. Her teeth chattered and she whimpered as her whole body trembled violently, shaking through already inflamed joints and her thumping head.

'Shh,' Alessandro murmured as he rhythmically rubbed her back and arm. 'Shh.'

She tried to snuggle closer. Tried to press as much of herself against him as possible, tried to become absorbed into him, into his heat, into his vitality. 'So c-cold.'

'Roll onto your other side,' Alessandro murmured.

Nat protested but he was moving and turning her gently, his hand on her hip, and with his help she rolled over. And then he was wrapping himself around her, spooning her, pulling her into his big warm chest, covering her limbs with his and plastering himself to every square inch of exposed skin.

It felt heavenly and she almost groaned out loud. She felt him kiss her hair and she nestled closer. Somewhere beneath the fever and the chills and the aches and pains she knew it was wrong but frankly she was too sick to care and as the rigor held her in its grip she'd never been more thankful to be held.

Nat wasn't sure of time and place when she woke alone the next morning. The curtains were drawn, only a few rays of sunlight finding the gaps. It took a few seconds to realise she was in Alessandro's bed and the memory of him holding her, spooning with her, in the middle of the night returned in a rush.

She looked over her shoulder to see the bedside clock. Her neck was stiff and her head felt all fuzzy, like she'd been given a lobotomy in the middle of the night and her skull stuffed with cotton wool.

Ten a.m.

'Ah, you're awake.'

Nat rolled on her back. He was standing in the doorway in shorts and T-shirt, his hair ruffled, his jaw dark with stubble.

'How are you feeling?'

'Like I've been run over by a truck.' Her mouth was dry and she licked her lips.

'Fancy some breakfast?'

Her stomach revolted at the very thought. 'Just some water.' She ran her tongue across her teeth. 'And a toothbrush.'

Alessandro grinned as he entered the room. 'Here are your next lot of pills. Why don't you take them, get up, have a shower and come back to bed?'

A shower sounded like bliss but just stretching her legs was a challenge. They felt like someone had been punching them repeatedly all night. She looked in the direction of her bedroom and doubted she could walk that far. 'I'm not sure I'm up to the trek.'

'Use my en suite. I'll get you some fresh clothes.'

He'd gone before she could answer and she was too weary to argue. It was, after all, the most sensible suggestion. And it wasn't like it was un-charted territory for her.

She shuffled to the side of the bed and slowly sat upright. A wave of light-headedness assaulted her and she shut her eyes until the dizziness passed. She downed the tablets and then stood gingerly on rubber legs, walking slowly to the shower.

Nat felt as weak as a newborn foal standing beneath the water and knew despite the luxury of the spray needling her skin she wouldn't be able to stay there for long. She leaned against the tiles, made a paltry attempt at throwing soap in all the right places and then shut off the taps.

She poked her head out of the screen and found a towel and clean pyjamas, even a pair of knick-ers hanging over the rail. She leaned against the vanity as she dried and dressed, her gaze falling on her toothbrush sitting next to Alessandro's.

She reached for it, catching a glimpse of herself in the mirror. She looked exactly like she felt, like a wrung-out dish mop. Pale, drawn, dark circles under her dull eyes, hair hanging limply around her face.

Her body was starting to ache again as she exited the bathroom, holding onto the walls for support. The freshly made-up bed was close but seemed light years away suddenly. She practically crawled to it and sank gratefully into its cool depths, utterly exhausted.

The aroma of clean linen filled her nostrils and on an empty stomach it was quite dizzying. She vaguely marvelled at the domesticity of it all. Toothbrushes side by side, clean sheets, her water glass topped up. If she hadn't been so weary it might have depressed the hell out of her, but it was nothing more than a fleeting thought before sleep once again sucked her under.

A few hours later Alessandro climbed the stairs to check on his patient. He'd just come off the phone from St Auburn's, who had confirmed that Nat had indeed contracted swamp flu. Thankfully both his and Juliano's swabs were so far negative.

She was due some more tablets and he thought she might like to know. He pulled up short in the doorway when he realised Juliano, Flo in tow, was propped up on the pillow next to Nat, chatting away. Her eyes were closed but that didn't seem to be bothering him.

He opened his mouth to motion for Juliano to come away but then his son said something that rendered him totally powerless.

'Please get better, Nat. I want you to be my mummy.' Juliano stroked Nat's forehead gently. 'We love you Nat.'

Alessandro's heart thundered in his chest as his son's innocent comments. Nat stirred at that point and murmured, 'Love you too, matey,' before settling back to sleep.

Alessandro held his breath. Was she lucid? Had she heard Juliano? He wasn't sure. A roaring in his ears threatened to deafen him as his chest filled with a feeling he was becoming all too used to. Except now he knew what it was.

All that he cared about in the world was right in front of him and he'd been so blind.

He was in love with Nathalie.

He'd been so busy punishing himself for past mistakes he hadn't been paying attention to what was happening in the here and now. When Nat had mentioned the 'l' word he'd run a mile because he'd still been looking back. But looking at his son and the woman in his bed—pale and ill and the best thing that had ever happened to him—he knew they were the way forward. He knew they were his future.

If it wasn't too late.

CHAPTER ELEVEN

NAT slept for the rest of the day, waking only for water, medication and the odd rest stop. She took the news of the confirmed diagnosis with a sleepy shrug and a 'Nice to know I'm a World Health Organization statistic now'.

Alessandro was pleased for the time. It gave him time to think, to strategise. He knew he had his work cut out for him. He knew that she'd been betrayed by two men in her past over another woman and that this time round she wouldn't be so forgiving. He knew she wouldn't take any platitudes or settle for any slick proclamations.

He was going to have to tell her the truth. The whole truth. Something he'd never told anyone. What was that old saying? The truth will set you free. Maybe it would. He hoped so. Maybe it was time to get it all out in the open instead of keeping it inside and beating himself up about it.

Surely he deserved love too? Juliano certainly

did. He knew he couldn't let her walk out of his life without trying. Hiding in the past hadn't done either of them any good. Maybe it was time to start looking forward, to start living for the future?

Alessandro came to bed late again that night, having gone over and over in his head what he was going to say to her once she was well enough. He was nervous, a sick kind of feeling sitting heavily in his stomach, like a layer of grease, sludgy and stagnant.

She didn't stir when he joined her and he turned on his side and just looked at her. He wanted to reach out for her, pull her into him as he had last night, but resisted. He wouldn't take advantage of her. Not when her defences had been knocked flat.

But he hoped she'd allow him to share her bed every night of his life. If he played his cards right maybe she would.

On that positive note he drifted to sleep

Nat woke with a start early next morning. Again it took a while to orientate herself as a pale finger of daylight peeked through the gap in the curtains.

Alessandro's room. She became aware of him behind her, wrapped around her again, his strong forearm so close to her cheek she could have turned her face and pressed a kiss to it.

Had she sought him out like the previous night or had it just been a natural position for their bodies to assume? The lovers within finding a way to be together if only subconsciously?

She realised suddenly she actually felt quite good. She wriggled slightly. No aches or pains. Her headache had gone and her thought processes didn't seem sluggish. She didn't feel feverish and her throat no longer hurt. She certainly couldn't run a marathon but it seemed as if the worse had passed.

She wriggled again for the sheer joy of being able to do so without pain and suddenly became aware of a hardness pressing into her from behind. And she knew instantly it was what had woken her, as surely as she knew her own heartbeat. The lover inside had subconsciously responded to the signal from her beloved.

'Alessandro?' she whispered.

Alessandro, who had been awake for fifteen minutes trying to quell his hard-on without waking her up, groaned behind her. He placed his forehead against her shoulder blade. 'I'm sorry, *il mio amore*. My body betrays me.'

A rush of desire slammed down low and she squeezed her legs together as a burst of heat tingled between them. He sounded in agony and she could definitely relate.

Alessandro took a deep steadying breath. 'If you let go of my arm, I'll get up.'

Nat realised his lower arm was trapped against her body. But suddenly she didn't want to release him. They'd forged a new kind of intimacy the last couple of days and she didn't want to let it go—not yet. She wanted to feel him around her, in her. Like before. Like old times.

Maybe her illness had weakened her but suddenly her blood was boiling with lust. His aroma filled her senses and the lust surged around her body, filling up every cell, every heartbeat, every breath. It was crazy, she knew, but was it so wrong to want one last moment with him to cherish for ever?

She reached behind her and slid her hand between them, seeking and finding his taut erection straining against his underwear.

Alessandro shut his eyes, pressing his forehead hard against her. 'Nathalie!' he groaned.

She gave him a fierce squeeze before burrowing past his waistband and touching his naked length, revelling in his guttural moan that echoed around the room. He sounded like a bull elephant in rut and she could barely see she was so inflamed with need.

She grabbed his lower hand and brought it to her breast, crying out herself as he squeezed it. 'Yes!'

'Nat…' Alessandro dragged in a breath as her hand slid up and down his length, sliding it enticingly against the cheek of her bottom. 'I don't think we should be doing this now. You're not well.'

Nat shook her head as his hand rubbed against the tortured peak of her nipple. 'I'm fine. I need this, Alessandro.' She moved her hand off him to push up her nightdress and shimmy her knickers down over her hips. She pressed her bare bottom back into him, rotating it against his erection.

'Nathalie!'

She reached for him again, wrapping her hand around his girth. 'Please.'

Alessandro was seeing stars in his efforts to hold back his desire while his body betrayed him. There was so much he wanted to tell her but he couldn't now. Not in the middle of all this.

She would think it was just pillow talk. Things people who didn't love each other said in bed that weren't necessarily true. And he didn't want to diminish what he had to say.

But he could show her. He could make love to her. Show her with his body, his touch, that she was more than sex, more than a substitute.

His hand left her nipple and she whimpered. 'Shh,' he said, kissing her neck. 'Just for a moment.' His fingers dragged up her nightdress so he could touch her warm vital flesh. The nipple was hard against his palm and as his other hand slid between her legs her arched back told him he'd definitely hit the sweet spot.

'Now, Alessandro. I need you in me now.'

Alessandro's hand stroked in unison. 'Slow down,' he whispered.

Nat shook her head. 'No.' She knew she was ready for him and she rubbed her hot slickness against his rampant hardness. She stretched her arm over her head, slinging it around his neck. 'Now,' she demanded.

Alessandro removed his hand reluctantly from between her legs and guided himself to where she was wet and hot for him. He nudged his head in, angling his hips at the same time she pushed back, and he slid in to the hilt.

Nat cried out at his decisive invasion, revelling in his thickness, his power. He pulled out and thrust in again as he squeezed her breast and she cried out, 'More.'

Alessandro's other hand returned to the wet cleft between her legs, her corresponding whimper travelling straight to his groin. Her hand tightened on his nape as he stroked between her legs and he dropped his head and bit gently along the length of her neck.

Her whimpers grew more frantic as he thrust deeper and stroked harder. Every frenzied noise drove him towards his own release. As she built he built too until she was trembling and clinging to him, crying out. When she shattered around him his own climax was tingling in his loins and surging through his abdominal muscles, rushing up to meet hers seconds later.

'I love you,' he called as the world fell apart around him.

Alessandro's unexpected declaration floated up to her in the surreal surroundings into which she had been flung. Maybe he hadn't even said it? Maybe her post-feverish brain had just conjured it up in her strangely inert yet somehow gliding state. She let it pass her by, not wanting to interfere with the slow burn of ecstasy fizzing in her blood.

It seemed to take for ever to bump gently back to earth, like feathers on a gentle breeze.

'Nathalie.' Alessandro nuzzled her neck, his hand resting possessively on her hip. 'We need to talk.'

No, she didn't want to hear him trying to back-pedal or justify his orgasmic slip. She just wanted to stay cocooned here for a bit longer, his arm around her, his body jammed tight against hers.

'Shh,' she whispered, tucking his arm snugly around her waist. 'Later.'

Then post-coital malaise and post-illness lethargy combined in a potent double whammy and sleep dragged her under.

It was full daylight when Nat next woke. The clock said six-thirty and her bladder was making itself known so she gently moved out of Alessandro's embrace. It was good to feel her legs strong beneath her as she padded to the en suite. Her stomach growled and she actually felt hungry for the first time in two days.

Alessandro's *I love you* played through her head as she used the toilet and then washed her hands. How could it not? She looked at her rather wan reflection, admitting to herself now how much it had hurt. Another pretty lie. Something he'd thought she wanted to hear.

Which she did, of course. But not if he didn't mean it. Not if he didn't feel it.

She steeled herself to go back out. To face him. To excuse what had happened with a cheery smile and get through the next few days with it firmly plastered on her face. Being ill had sapped her energy. And being angry required more energy than she possessed. She just wanted it to be over now so she could leave and lick her wounds far away from the man who had inflicted them.

He was sitting on the side of the bed, waiting for her when she stepped out of the en suite. Her gaze hungrily ate up his broad shoulders and his long, bare, powerful thighs.

'We need to talk.'

Nat faltered. Wanting to prolong their nearness, to hear his voice but not wanting it at the same time. 'It's okay. You don't have to explain, Alessandro.' She looked at the floor then at the bed then at the bedside clock. 'I'm not going to hold you to anything you might have said in a moment of passion.'

Alessandro caught her wandering gaze and held it. 'I love you.'

Nat shook her head, rejecting his words, the sincerity in his gaze. 'It was a nice thing for you to say but you really didn't have to and I understand where it came from.'

Alessandro prayed for patience. 'I love you,' he said again.

Nat refused to let his words affect her. Rob had said he loved her. So had her father. Neither of them had stuck around. 'No. You're still in love and grieving for your wife. And I remind you of her. I think they call it transference, don't they?'

Alessandro pushed off the bed and stalked two paces to the window, yanking back the curtain. This was the moment of truth. He placed his fists against the window ledge, the persuasive words he'd practised yesterday completely deserting him.

All he had now was the bald truth. 'I didn't love her.'

The silence stretched as Nat tried to figure out what he was talking about. She frowned. Who the hell were they talking about now? 'Who?'

'Camilla. My wife. I didn't love her.' The words he'd kept locked inside for so long were finally out and damn if it didn't feel good. He turned to face her, leaning against the window sill. 'I never loved her.'

Nat blinked. 'What?' But the man she'd first met had been deeply mired in grief.

'You're right,' he admitted. 'You and she are very similar. I was shocked when I first met you. But it took me about two seconds in your company to realise that your physical similarities are where it ends. When I told you that you and she were nothing alike, I was deadly serious.'

Nat wasn't sure if her brain was still sluggish from her illness but she just couldn't take in what he was saying. 'I don't understand.'

'Camilla was my lover. Before we met I was having a fantastic time playing the field. I never planned to marry. You grow up with parents who fought and spent more time apart than together, you don't really see the point…'

Alessandro couldn't believe he'd ever been so stupid. 'She was beautiful and sophisticated, from aristocratic stock. Witty and charming and looked fantastic naked. All the things I looked for in a date. And then she fell pregnant. So I did the honourable thing.'

He paused waiting for the burn of bitter memories. For his internal censor to step in. But neither came.

A first.

'It was a huge society wedding and I was determined to make a real go of it. So, my life hadn't gone exactly according to plan but I knew if we worked at it, we could succeed.'

He shook his head at his naivety. 'Valentino, who, I have to say, never really liked her anyway, overheard her at the wedding talking to her best friend about how she'd trapped me. Deliberately fallen pregnant because she'd wanted to marry me. I told him he was mistaken and confronted her about it later, in the honeymoon suite.'

His lips twisted into an ironic smile. 'She admitted it. She looked straight at me and said, *"But, darling, you wouldn't have married me otherwise."* It was like the blinkers had been ripped away from my eyes and I could finally see the person Val had always seen. The cold, calculating socialite out to marry a doctor.'

Nat watched him closely as Alessandro fell silent, his matter-of-fact retelling betrayed by the turmoil in his sable gaze. To say she was horrified was an understatement. 'I didn't know,' she murmured.

He nodded. 'So I told her it was going to be a

marriage in name only. Which apparently suited her down to the ground. Initially anyway. So we entered into this strange existence where we smiled publicly but slept in separate beds. And then Juliano was born and I was crazily busy at the hospital, working long hours, and she suddenly realised being married to a doctor wasn't so glamorous after all.'

He gave a stiff laugh. 'I think she thought I'd give up the emergency lark and become a Harley St specialist.'

Nat shook her head. She'd known Alessandro for only a matter of days when she'd realised he was a gifted emergency physician.

'She wanted a divorce. But she wanted me to file. Couldn't have that stain on her family's reputation. I knew I'd never see Juliano again if I agreed. As it was, she was already using him to get to me. Don't get me wrong, she was a great mother and they had a close bond but she deliberately alienated him from me. Rationing our already scant time together. Insisting I only speak English with him. And...I let her. I felt guilty about our relationship and it was easier to give in and play by her rules. Juliano was happy and healthy and loved. And work demanded so much of me. It was easier that way. I guess I turned into my father...'

He trailed off and Nat waited for him to start again. She sensed this was something he needed to get off his chest.

'By the time she died, Juliano and I were relative strangers.'

Nat nodded. 'I noticed.' She sat down on the edge of the bed. 'How did she die?'

'A car accident. We'd argued and she'd squealed off in the flash BMW she insisted I buy for her—another guilt gift.'

Nat shut her eyes. No wonder Alessandro had looked so wretched when she'd first met him. He obviously blamed himself for Camilla's death. Guilt and remorse were powerful emotions. 'What did you argue about?'

'The divorce. What else? We didn't argue often, I didn't want that for Juliano. I didn't want him to experience the type of childhood I'd known. It was easier just to give in to her. And Camilla was much too passive-aggressive for it anyway.'

He swallowed, parched from talking and the burn of memories. 'But we rowed that day. I couldn't believe I was in a marriage like my parents'. But Camilla had a way of picking a fight.'

The ugly words taunted him to this day. 'She said she'd taken a lover and wanted to be free to marry again. I told her over my cold dead body and that I would fight her every inch of the way. Fight her for Juliano. That she'd made her bed and she was just going to have to lie in it.'

He went silent and Nat finished the story for him. 'So she hared off in the car and crashed it?'

Alessandro nodded and her heart went out to him. She rose from the bed and went to his side, leaning her body in to him, pressing a kiss to his shoulder. 'It wasn't your fault, Alessandro.'

'I know that. Rationally, I know that. But...'

Nat nodded, dropping another kiss in the same spot. 'You've been beating yourself up about it anyway?'

Alessandro felt the warmth of her seep into him and he began to hope. 'I looked on it as my punishment. For insisting on a marriage on paper only and then for keeping her in the marriage. A marriage neither of us wanted. If I'd only forgiven her and gone on from there. Tried to make a real go of it instead of drawing the battle lines right from the start. But I was proud and angry.'

'It must have been hard.'

Yes, it had. But, then, a lot of it had been his doing.

'So you see,' he said, looking down at her, 'I don't deserve to have love, to find love. That's why I fought these feelings for you for so long. Because this isn't supposed to be my lot. And then I saw Juliano in bed with you yesterday. You were asleep and he was stroking your head and telling you he wanted you to be his mummy and he loved you and you murmured, "I love you too," and I realised that right in front of me was my whole world. You and him.'

Nat didn't remember Juliano being in bed with her but smiled at the picture Alessandro painted. Her heart started to beat crazily as his words sank in. She wanted to believe him. But she was burned and wary.

She looked up and captured his gaze. 'I just can't get her picture out of my head.'

'I know. I should have told you earlier but I honestly didn't notice the resemblance after being in your company for just a few seconds. You were obviously like chalk and cheese.'

He lifted a finger and stroked it down her face.

'It's you I want. And not because you look like Camilla. Because you're Nat. Nathalie. Our Nat. Funny and down to earth and kind and generous and sexy, and you gave me back my son, you gave me back Juliano, and you opened my heart enough to see that maybe I do deserve a chance at love. Real love for the first time in my life.'

Nat's chest bloomed with an outpouring of the love that she'd kept firmly in check since she'd blurted it out. 'Of course you do, Alessandro. We all do.'

Alessandro saw the compassion in her gaze and dared to hope. 'Does this mean I haven't destroyed everything you felt for me?' he asked.

She smiled up at him, her heart skipping in her chest. She slipped her palm up to cradle his cheek. 'Of course not. I love you, Alessandro. I can't turn that off and on. It's a fact of life. It's who I am.'

She raised herself up on tiptoe and pressed her mouth to his. 'I will always love you.'

Alessandro grinned for the first time since he'd started talking. Then he picked her up, ignoring her squeal, and threw her in the centre of the mattress. 'So you'll stay,' he said, climbing on the bed and lying beside her on his stomach, propped up on his elbows. 'For ever and ever. And you'll marry me and have brothers and sisters for Juliano?'

She put her arms around his neck. 'Yes, I'll stay. Yes, I'll marry you. And, yes, I'll have brothers and sisters for Juliano.' She pulled him down to seal it with a kiss. 'You want to start now?'

Alessandro grinned. 'I thought we did that already.'

A noise at the door had them both breaking apart as Juliano eyed them. 'Is Nat better now?'

Alessandro grinned at his son. 'She sure is. And guess what?' he said, gesturing Juliano over. He grabbed his son's hand and pulled him onto the bed with them. 'Nat's staying. For ever.'

Juliano's eyes grew large in his head as he looked from his father to Nat and back to his father. 'Really? Are you going to be my mummy?'

Nat beamed at him. 'Would you like that?'

'Oh, yeah! That'd be the best thing ever,' he said enthusiastically, bouncing up and down on his haunches.

Alessandro couldn't have agreed more. 'Well said, matey.' He grinned as he grabbed Juliano and lifted him in the air above his head, tickling him with his fingers, boyish laughter filling the room.

Nat laughed too as Juliano giggled and begged his father to stop. She pinched herself. She was really a part of all this. She couldn't remember every being this deliriously happy.

It couldn't get any better than this.

But it did.

MEDICAL™

Large Print ✓

Titles for the next six months…

April

✓ BACHELOR OF THE BABY WARD	Meredith Webber
✓ FAIRYTALE ON THE CHILDREN'S WARD	Meredith Webber
✓ PLAYBOY UNDER THE MISTLETOE	Joanna Neil
✓ OFFICER, SURGEON…GENTLEMAN!	Janice Lynn
✓ MIDWIFE IN THE FAMILY WAY	Fiona McArthur
✓ THEIR MARRIAGE MIRACLE	Sue MacKay

May

✓ DR ZINETTI'S SNOWKISSED BRIDE	Sarah Morgan
✓ THE CHRISTMAS BABY BUMP	Lynne Marshall
✓ CHRISTMAS IN BLUEBELL COVE	Abigail Gordon
✓ THE VILLAGE NURSE'S HAPPY-EVER-AFTER	Abigail Gordon
✓ THE MOST MAGICAL GIFT OF ALL	Fiona Lowe
✓ CHRISTMAS MIRACLE: A FAMILY	Dianne Drake

June

✓ ST PIRAN'S: THE WEDDING OF THE YEAR	Caroline Anderson
✓ ST PIRAN'S: RESCUING PREGNANT CINDERELLA	Carol Marinelli
✓ A CHRISTMAS KNIGHT	Kate Hardy
✓ THE NURSE WHO SAVED CHRISTMAS	Janice Lynn
✓ THE MIDWIFE'S CHRISTMAS MIRACLE	Jennifer Taylor
✓ THE DOCTOR'S SOCIETY SWEETHEART	Lucy Clark

MEDICAL™

Large Print

July

SHEIKH, CHILDREN'S DOCTOR...HUSBAND   Meredith Webber

SIX-WEEK MARRIAGE MIRACLE   Jessica Matthews

RESCUED BY THE DREAMY DOC   Amy Andrews

NAVY OFFICER TO FAMILY MAN   Emily Forbes

ST PIRAN'S: ITALIAN SURGEON,   Margaret McDonagh
FORBIDDEN BRIDE

THE BABY WHO STOLE THE DOCTOR'S HEART   Dianne Drake

August

CEDAR BLUFF'S MOST ELIGIBLE BACHELOR   Laura Iding

DOCTOR: DIAMOND IN THE ROUGH   Lucy Clark

BECOMING DR BELLINI'S BRIDE   Joanna Neil

MIDWIFE, MOTHER...ITALIAN'S WIFE   Fiona McArthur

ST PIRAN'S: DAREDEVIL, DOCTOR...DAD!   Anne Fraser

SINGLE DAD'S TRIPLE TROUBLE   Fiona Lowe

September

SUMMER SEASIDE WEDDING   Abigail Gordon

REUNITED: A MIRACLE MARRIAGE   Judy Campbell

THE MAN WITH THE LOCKED AWAY HEART   Melanie Milburne

SOCIALITE...OR NURSE IN A MILLION?   Molly Evans

ST PIRAN'S: THE BROODING HEART SURGEON   Alison Roberts

PLAYBOY DOCTOR TO DOTING DAD   Sue MacKay

MILLS & BOON™